KINGDOM COME

KEYS TO THE KINGDOM PREQUEL

Limited Edition Novella

KINGDOM COME

KEYS TO THE KINGDOM
PREQUEL

TY MARSHALL

KINGDOM COME

WWW.TYMARSHALLBOOKS.COM

BOOK AND COVER DESIGN BY JOSHUA WIRTH
ISBN: 978-0-9984419-5-5

FIRST EDITION: OCT 2018
10 9 8 7 6 5 4 3 2 1

Ty Marshall

Kingdom Come

CHAPTER 1

New York City, 1978

The Greyhound bus sailed northbound on Interstate 95, making its way through New Jersey. Marion rode in silence, occasionally taking in the passing scenery but mostly he just stared at his own reflection in the mirror. The fourteen-hour ride from Fayetteville, North Carolina to New York City was nearing its end but by the look on his face you couldn't tell if he was happy or not. His mind was preoccupied by heavy thoughts. He had entered the army as a raw seventeen-year old hoping to experience the world. Now, almost four years later, he was returning as a hardened young man that had seen a bit too much. A natural leader, Marion was already equipped with tons of street savvy but the army had provided him with an education that he couldn't get anywhere else. They had trained him to kill, then sent him to Vietnam to slaughter without consequence. The United States government then told him, he was free to go back home, where he was expected to flip the off switch and live a regular life. Back to the "Rotten Apple," filled with worms and warts; dealers, thieves and murderers. But Marion didn't see the city that way, he saw nothing but opportunity. He was highly intelligent and strategic; planning every move and counter move like a chess player. With his calm demeanor and easy charm, he was ready for his own slice of the "Big Apple," he just had one piece of unfinished business to handle. Marion looked down at the piece of paper he held in his hand. It was small, barely big enough to fit the name and address scribbled on it. He repeated both to himself then smirked with eager anticipation as the bus crossed the George Washington Bridge and entered New York.

A few minutes later, the bus was pulling into the terminal. When it came to a stop, Marion wasted no time grabbing his bags and exited along with the other passengers. Once off the bus, he inhaled deeply, enjoying the fresh air after hours of breathing in stale bus air. He stretched his arms and legs, then began to take in the sights and sounds of the city. The streets were busy with cars and the sidewalks were packed with people moving in different directions. Marion missed being home and stared up at the buildings like it was his first time in the big city. Anybody passing by could have easily mistaken him for a tourist at that moment.

Suddenly, he heard someone calling his name in the distance, followed by the honking of a car horn. He turned towards the adjoining street, where a car was double parked with someone's waving hand hanging outside the driver's side window. Cautious by nature, Marion slowly approached, shielding his eyes from the sun as he tried to get a clearer view. When he got a few feet away, a man leaped from behind the steering wheel and charged at Marion with a wide grin on his face and his arms stretched out wide. A look of recognition appeared on Marion's face and he dropped his bag preparing for the embrace.

"Got damn nigga, look at you. It's good to see you again," Goose said. His voice was naturally loud but not in a brash way. Goose was light skin, tall and lanky with a long neck that had earned him his nickname, he had big bugged eyes that darted back and forth like he was searching for something. He and Marion were members of the same street gang coming up, The Ace of Spades.

"Nigga, it's good to be seen," Marion admitted as the two old pals hugged briefly. "How you been?" he asked.

"Good, good, really good," Goose repeated with excitement before his voice shifted to a more serious tone. "How was it over there? A lotta cats coming back from over there like zombies or something, just different," Goose asked as he looked Marion in the eye.

"War changes a muthafucka," Marion said calmly, downplaying the depths of the things he had witnessed. "What's everybody been up too?" he changed the subject by asking about the old gang he had left behind when he joined the army.

To say Marion "joined" the army was a bit of a stretch. He really didn't have much of a choice. He was facing jail time for his part in a fight with a rival gang that resulted in a rival gang member's death. While being held in central bookings, an army recruiter came to visit the jailed teenager and offered him a chance to have his case dismissed. All Marion had to do was enlist and after four years of service it would be like his troubles never happened. The chance had been offered to all being held in the jail that night. Most turned their nose up at the recruiter, clowning and laughing at him. All except Marion, who after giving it some thought took the opportunity, longing for the chance to see more than just the ghettos of the inner city.

Goose dropped his eyes. "Maaan, cats are all over the place these days. Some doin' good, some not," he replied. "Some of the niggas we ran with, out here ridin' that white horse. Others, the horse is ridin' them," he explained to Marion about the effects the heroin game had on the rest of the Aces.

"What's the word on Bank?" Marion asked.

"Shit, dat nigga Bank pimpin' hard. He gotta big ol' pretty Cadillac and some prettier hoes," Goose bragged. "He ain't fuckin' with no dope."

Marion smiled and nodded. "Got damn, Goose, who's left?"

Goose chuckled. "I gotta few guys. A couple young thoroughbreds that got down after you left," he explained. He immediately saw the skepticism in Marion's face and tried to reassure him. "Trust me they're solid. I vouch for them," he placed his hand over his heart expressing his sincerity.

"So they're ready?" Marion asked.

"Yeah, just waiting on you," Goose said confidently.

Marion nodded and didn't say another word about it as they walked towards the car.

* * *

Marion stood on the sidewalk soaking in the scene. A lot had changed about the old neighborhood. There was a parade of prowling prostitutes up and down the block and tons of junkies were littered directly across the street waiting to cop their fix. Renegade dealers raced to every car that pulled up on the block, sticking their hands in the windows trying to make a sell. What was once a controlled operation had turned into an open drug market, a free for all and Marion saw the lack of organization as his way in.

Goose noticed that look in his eyes. "Told you nigga, it's a lotta bread coming through here," he said.

"You was right," Marion agreed in his deep, calm baritone voice. "But the way they doing it, this shit ain't gon' last too much longer."

"C'mon," Goose said tapping him on the arm. "Let me introduce you to a couple cats."

Nelle's Bar used to be the main hangout for members of The Aces and still was for what was left of the gang. Goose led the way as they entered the bar and walked through thick clouds of cigarette smoke. Parliament's "Flashlight" blared from the jukebox as a group of women danced up against the wall. A beautiful brown skin fox stared directly at Marion with sexual lust in her eyes. She flashed an inviting smile but he didn't acknowledge her as he kept it moving following Goose to the bar. It had been a minute since he had been with a woman, the jungles of Vietnam weren't the place to have your mind on anything other than surviving. The woman had peaked his interest more than he cared to admit but he had more important things to take care of at the moment. That was Marion, all business, all the time. He hadn't even been home a full 24 hours and was already tending to business and putting things in motion.

A man sitting on a stool quickly got up when he saw

Goose approaching, allowing him to slide into the opening at the bar.

"Josie!" Goose called out to the shapely women behind the bar with her back to him. "Look what the cat done drug in."

"Oh my God!" Josie screamed as she turned and saw Marion standing there. She raced over to the bar and hugged him tightly around his neck. "Look at you," she raved. He had physically matured since she had last seen him. He was slightly taller with broader shoulders and his athletic frame was now rock solid like concrete. He had an air of confidence about himself and his brown eyes seemed to lack any fear. As he flashed his pearly white smile, she thought to herself that he was even more handsome now than she remembered.

"What's going on cuz? It's good to see you." Marion said hugging her back. They were about the same age and had been the closest of friends growing up in the Williamsburg section of Brooklyn. The Killing Field as it was called, was known for its high crime rate, harboring both violent street gang activity and organized crime. Marion's knuckle game quickly helped build his reputation after being sent to live in the projects with his aunt, Josie's mother, following his father being shipped off to prison. Over the years Josie had become more like a sister to him than a cousin. He always protected her and they had a strong, loving bond that had formed early in their childhood.

"I can't believe it's really you," she said searching him over making sure he had returned from the war with all his parts.

"In the flesh," he replied. "Did you get my letters?" he asked.

"Every one of 'em," she answered.

"Did you take care of what I asked?"

Josie smiled and walked over to the cash register. She opened it then lifted up the cash tray, removing something. She walked back over to Marion and handed him a set of keys to the apartment he told her to get for him. "Have I ever let you down?" she asked.

"Not once." Marion answered. "Wish I could say the same for ya man here," he cracked pointing at Goose.

"Husband," Goose corrected as Josie's smile widened and she flashed the modest diamond on her finger.

"Since when?" a surprised Marion asked.

"Couple of months now," Josie said.

"Congratulations," he said with a big smile then hugged her again.

"Let's have a couple drinks to celebrate," she said.

"In a minute," Marion explained. "Goose was just about to introduce me to a few people. Ain't that right...cuz," he reminded his old friend.

"Yeah, that's right," Goose said. "They're over here."

Marion followed him over to a group gathered around a couple pool tables. They were a motley crew of characters; light, dark, short, tall but the one thing Marion noticed that they all had in common was their baby faces. Not one of them looked older than seventeen or eighteen. Goose could feel Marion's icy glare fall on him before he even began to introduce him to the group.

"Hey fellas, listen up," Goose's voice boomed grabbing the groups attention. "This the nigga I been telling y'all about, "The" Marion Holloway."

All knew the name, his reputation amongst The Aces was solidified even with the new members. Marion could see the admiration in their eyes as he shook each members hand. He was an original member of the gang. The young men looked at him like a legend, although he was just a few years older than most of them. Unbeknownst to all in attendance, this was where the real legend of Marion Holloway would begin. The young men remained quiet, eager to hear what he had to say.

"Who do those niggas out there, work for?" Marion asked looking over at Goose.

"Nobody really," Goose answered.

"Nobody?" Marion asked. "Who's supplying them then?"

"Depends," Goose explained. "Most of the shit has been through a few hands by the time them niggas out there get it. But the source of the dope is a big time cat out of Harlem named Charles Matthews."

"Charlie Hustle," one of the young men said. "Word is, he got a mean connect wit' some Cubans or Colombians, something like that. He got the purest dope in the city."

"Who does he answer to?" Marion asked.

"Nobody. He runs Harlem. The head nigga in charge," Goose said with extra emphasis on the word nigga. "There's another boss, an Italian named Martello, who's been trying to muscle in on him; but for the most part Charlie controls everything from 110th to 155th Street, Lenox Ave to Broadway."

Marion nodded. "Listen," he said as he began to address

the gang. "We were once the strongest force in this neighborhood, outside of the mob. But the days of gangbanging, fist fighting in the streets have come and gone. It's time we get organized and get some real business about ourselves. First thing that needs to go are these," he said pointing at a slim built young man sporting a cut off jean jacket with The Ace of Spades patch on it.

"What you mean?" the young man questioned. "I earned my patch. People know what it represents when they see it. They know to respect me," he said proudly.

"Real gangsters move in silence," Marion explained. "That patch right there let's everybody know your business, including the police. From now on it's nothing but slacks and dress shoes, suits and silk threads. You gotta dress for success. Can't make no real money dressing like a common criminal, ya dig?"

"Speaking of real money," a barrel chested teenager named Sonny spoke up. He was seen as the neighborhood tough guy, standing over six feet tall with arms and legs like tree trunks. He was all muscle and no brains. "How we supposed to get this real money you talkin' about? Shit, ain't none of us got no connections. We just nickelin' and dimin' like the rest of them niggas out there. How you suppose to change that?"

"You let me worry about that. You just be ready when the time comes," Marion said firmly. The group fell silent once again. Marion didn't let anyone in on his exact plan but he spoke with such confidence that it made them all willing to follow him, even Sonny. After a few seconds, Marion smiled then looked from the teenagers to Goose and said, "Alright, let's make some fuckin' money."

CHAPTER 2

Harlem, New York

It was not yet noon but already humid as hundreds of shoppers crowded the sidewalks of 125th Street. The strip was home to shops of all kinds, from fish markets and fruit stands, to restaurants and elaborate clothing stores. The *World Famous* Apollo Theater sat in the middle of the bustling block and provided live entertainment for the mostly impoverished locals. The marquee on the building read that *The O'Jays* would be performing tonight. Vendors were full of energy, dashing back and forth making their best sales pitch, hoping shoppers would take the bait and spend money with them. While many of the locals lingered on stoops preferring not to take part in the chaos and congestion on the street.

A few blocks over a blue Chevy Nova was parked on 127th and St. Nicholas with its tinted windows rolled up. Two men sat in the front seat with the engine idling and the air condition on blast trying to beat the heat. One, a slim faced Italian with a beak for a nose, was staring out the window with a laser like focus watching as the locals scurried up and down the block. The other sat behind the steering wheel resting his head against the soft leather headrest with his eyes closed, trying to shake off the effects of a long night with not enough sleep.

The first man removed a pack of Marlboro's from his pocket, put one in his mouth, lit it and tossed the pack on the dashboard. "When is this fucking guy supposed to show?" he asked cracking the window slightly and blowing out smoke.

"I know as much as you do Gino," the man behind the steering wheel said, his eyes still closed. "Maybe it's one of those things where the less we know, the better we are. I prefer it that way."

"Maybe," Gino said, "I'd just like to have a little more information, that's all."

The man behind the wheel opened his eyes and took a deep breath. He reached inside his jacket pulling out a picture. He passed it to his partner, "This is all you need to know," he said peering out the driver side window.

"Dammit," Gino said voicing his frustration. "How long have we been doing work for the Martello family? Since I was old enough to remember, I've been cracking heads, kidnapping and killing. And look at us, we're still no better than errand boys. When are they gonna open up the books for us huh?" He said voicing his frustration at not yet being a made man. "We're like orphans or some shit."

The driver shrugged his shoulders nonchalantly. "Maybe I didn't get into this expecting as much as you did Gino. I'm not looking to be attached to a family. I'm an independent contractor, work for hire. We are who we are and we're paid well to do what we do. I'm fine with that."

"Well I'm not!" Gino declared.

"Are you dumb or just stupid?" The driver questioned in his strong Italian accent as the thin features in his face lowered into a scowl. "What do you wanna be like these bums out here, the niggers?" He pointed out the window at a group of young men huddled on a corner. "Drinking fifths of cheap wine every day, selling small bags of heroin for pennies, barely making enough to afford the rent on the roach infested shitholes they live in. Looking up to that fuckin' hump," he said pointing at the picture in Gino's hand. "God of the ghetto," he snickered. "You make a good living Gino. You live in a nice house on Staten Island, your kids go to great schools and your wife shops whenever she friggin' wants. And you work a few times a month. What is there to complain about?"

Gino remained silent, shaking his head from left to right as he soaked up everything his old partner had to say.

"Exactly," the driver stated seeing he had made his point. "Now keep your friggin' eyes open and tell me when you see them," he commanded before closing his eyes once again.

* * *

Charles Matthews, or Charlie Hustle as he was called by everyone, was the toast of Harlem. A gangster and a gentleman who had managed to break the Italian Mob's control of the heroin and cocaine that flowed through his neighborhood. Besides controlling the sale of narcotics, his organization supplied other drug dealers throughout the East Coast. His goal was to unify all the major Black and Hispanic dealers around the country into an interdependent council called The Brotherhood that could rival The Commission. He knew fracturing the mob's control of drug importation meant he wouldn't have to rely on them for survival going forward. His way of thinking made him beloved by his peers but made him a sworn enemy of The Commission, who didn't want his ideology filtering through the underworld, threatening their power.

"I'm not doing business with none of those guinea bastards," he voiced to a small audience of his organization gathered in his den. Four of which were his brothers. A light cloud danced around him as the air slowly became more pungent from the Cuban cigar in his mouth. He looked like the boss, dressed dapper with a white shirt and suspenders holding up his grey pants. "I got a Cuban cat with a direct line to the Colombians out in Miami bringing dope in by the shit load. So much blow, they damn near giving it away," he bragged. "The price is more than fair and the product is pure as a catholic school girl. You tell me why would I ever consider doing business with the Italians. I got way better dope than that stepped on shit they're trying to force on everybody."

Charles's ambitious spirit wasn't foreign to his siblings. He had left Hattiesburg, Mississippi for New York City as a fresh faced teenager many years before with nothing but bus fare and some raggedy hair clippers. While working as a barber, his large and muscular build caught the eye of a local bookie who offered him a job as a collector and enforcer. Charles quickly grew tired of the numbers game but two things came from it that would change his fortunes forever. It earned him the connections and most importantly the cash he needed to enter the drug business. An elderly Cuban he met through the numbers game introduced him to a supplier and within a few months, he was a major player in the New York City dope game. The close relationship between Charles and the elderly Cuban spawned more than just a drug empire. Exceedingly fond of the young hustler, the man introduced his daughter to Charles and eventually gave his blessing when he decided to make her his wife.

On his rise to boss of Harlem, Charles learned a few important lessons from the old man before he passed. One being that the quiet, understated sophistication of his clothing would allow him to pass as a respectable businessman. While flashier rivals brought unnecessary attention to themselves and got picked off by the cops, Charles continued to thrive. Eventually he sent for his brothers, Pee-Wee, Zeke, Al and the youngest Jimmy, and together they took over Harlem.

A light knock on the sliding den doors caught everyone's attention and made Charles pause mid-sentence. "Who is it?" he called out.

"It's me, daddy," the angelic voice replied from the other side of the door.

"Come in baby," he answered.

The door slid open slowly and when it came to a stop, eighteen year old Emma stood in the doorway wearing a smile on her face. Charles beamed with pride at the sight of his beautiful daughter, she was the apple of his eye and a splitting image of her mother. His normal commanding and authoritative ways disappeared when she was in his presence. His tough exterior was no match for her. She was his weakness and everyone knew Emma had the big guy wrapped around her pretty little fingers.

"Hi everybody," she said playfully waving at the members of her father's organization who all turned and spoke to her. "Sorry to interrupt but how much longer are you gonna be daddy?" she pouted, poking out her lip. "You promised to take me shopping today."

"That I did," he acknowledged with a big grin. "Give daddy a few more minutes and we'll go."

"Arrh," she groaned under her breath so he couldn't hear. "Okay," she said sounding a little disappointed before turning on her heels and disappearing out of sight.

"She's the real boss of the family," Charles said smiling and shaking his head. "Well fellas, family duties call," he said clapping his hands and rubbing them together, signaling the end of the meeting.

A small group led by Charles and Emma spilled out of the brownstone and onto the street. The love Harlem had for Charles was immediately on display as people flocked to him as he strolled down the block. Old ladies waved to him from their windows and people called out to him from all over the block. He greeted them all with a wave or a head nod and a smile. He was the "Mayor of St. Nick" and Emma reveled in her father's celebrity. She was treated like royalty in the neighborhood. The boss's daughter was beloved by all. The only female flanked by a mob of well-dressed, powerful men, she resembled a queen with her queen's guard as she strutted down the city street.

Full of life and energy, Emma dipped in and out of every clothing store, dragging her father along for her retail adventure. Shopping was the thing she enjoyed doing most, even more than ballet which was her first love but she had slowly moved away from it after her mother died. Since a child, Emma loved shopping with her dad because he would always say yes to the expensive things her mom said no to, that hadn't changed. Distracted by Emma's frenetic pace, no one in the entourage noticed the car lurking as they sauntered down the street.

Finally, Charles decided he had enough, he refused to go into another store. They had been out long enough under the burning hot sun and he could see in his daughter's eyes that she had no plans on stopping anytime soon. "No mas," he said exhausted and fatigued.

"Daaaaddyyyy," Emma whined like a spoiled child trying to get her way. When that didn't work she put on a sad puppy dog face, cuffing her arm under his.

Charles knew there was no point in him resisting. "Ok, but this is the last one," he said. "Run in there with her," he instructed his brother Pee Wee, "And make sure she hurry up, man."

Charles watched with a few of his bodyguards as Emma and Pee Wee walked towards the store.

"Hey, Mr. Matthews can I shine your shoes?" A voice called out from behind him.

"What you say?" Charles asked as he turned seeing a young man standing close by.

"I said, can I shine your shoes Mr. Matthews sir," the young man repeated.

"I'm okay," Charles answered.

"Please Mr. Matthews, I'm just out here trying to make some money to buy me some school clothes," the young man who looked to be college age explained trying his hardest to sell his services.

Charles looked him up and down. The boy's dingy appearance and worn out shoes reminded Charles of when he was less fortunate. The oldest of five, he knew what it was like to go without. He looked back over his shoulder, Emma and Pee Wee had disappeared into another store.

"You know what," he said turning back towards the young man. "Today's your lucky day kid." Charles reached into his pocket and peeled off a hundred-dollar bill. "You better be good," he smiled before handing it to the young man.

"I promise you sir, it'll be the best you ever had," the energetic young man proclaimed taking the money.

"Okay," Charles said finally conceding to the request and taking a seat.

* * *

Emma entered the clothing store and immediately gave her uncle Pee Wee the eye. He burst into laughter, already knowing the routine. He posted up, waiting by the front door while Emma walked off to shop. Pee Wee was her favorite out of all of her uncles, mostly because he let her get away with murder. He knew his brother kept Emma under strict lock and key. He was sympathetic towards her so when they were together he was far more lenient with the rules.

"Do your unc a favor, baby girl. Don't be too long, ok?" Pee Wee called out to her.

Emma turned and saw a wide grin spread across Pee Wee's face. He knew no matter what he said, she was going to take her sweet time. "Ok," she said playing right along.

Emma strolled through the various sections of the

clothing store, browsing and picking out different outfits to try on. She had a bunch of clothes draped over her arm as she made her way towards the fitting rooms. When she arrived, she began searching around for an attendant to help her.

"Excuse me, do you work here," she called out to a man with his back turned to her.

Marion turned around ready to reply with a no but his words got caught in his throat momentarily. He couldn't believe his eyes. He had truly never seen a woman like the one standing in front of him. Her physical beauty was unmatched. The flawless, golden complexion of her skin looked to him like she had been kissed by the sun. Her black hair was thick, curly and flowed down over her shoulders.

"Yes, how may I help you?" he smoothly answered her question, trying to see where it would lead.

Emma's heart nearly skipped a beat in her chest when he turned to face her. She was instantly captivated by the salesman. He was outstandingly handsome and very masculine. His bronze skin was smooth and clear as a Summer's day. His perfect smile reeled her in and she quickly lost herself in his deep brown eyes. It was already too late when she realized that she was staring.

"I wanted to try on a few things," she said breaking from her trance.

"No problem," Marion played along. "The fitting room to your left should be open. I'll be right here if you need any help," he told her.

Emma turned and headed for the fitting room. She was blushing the whole time, feeling all giddy inside. She closed the door behind her, the good-looking stranger consuming all her thoughts. She began quickly sorting through the clothes she had picked out. Finding what she thought was the sexiest out of all of them, she undressed in a hurry then slipped into the new clothes.

"Excuse me," she called out while still getting dressed. "Are you still there?" she inquired to Marion.

"Yes, I'm right here," he called back to her with a smirk on his face.

"I wanted to know if you could give me your honest opinion on this outfit. I can't decide if I like it or not," Emma tried her best to sound innocent although she was openly flirting.

"Sure." Marion answered.

Emma cracked a big smile before exiting the fitting room

and strutting into view like she was on a runway. She was wearing a light pink chiffon sheath dress that only covered one of her shoulders. "Sooo," she asked as she tilted her head slightly.

Marion took a moment to appreciate her beauty. She had a model's face and a dancer's body, thin but shapely with legs that seemed to go on forever. Now it was his heart that was pounding in his chest. But his silence made Emma feel a bit self-conscious and she began to twist the ends of her hair, nervously, as it laid on her shoulder.

"Turn around," Marion said.

The confidence he spoke with made her oblige without any hesitation. She spun around slowly, giving him a full view that she hoped would last.

"I think it's perfect," he said. "The pink brings out the color in your eyes."

Emma stifled a giggle instead she just smiled. "Thank you," she paused waiting for him to tell her his name.

"Marion," he said. "And you are?"

"Emma," she replied.

"Nice meeting you Emma," he said extending his hand to her. She reached out and shook his hand. "Glad I could help but I really need to get back to work," he said still pretending to be a salesperson in the store.

"Nice meeting you too Marion. And thank you, again."

Emma placed her hand over her chest as she watched him walk away. The thought of his body on top of hers made her swoon for the first time in her life. There was such a sensation racing through her body that her knees buckled from the quiver in her panties. Emma broke from her trance and headed back to the fitting room to change.

Emma approached the register and placed the clothes she chose on the counter. Her uncle Pee Wee was relieved when he saw her. He was just as ready to go as her father had been minutes earlier.

"Did you find everything you needed," the cashier asked.

Emma wanted to scream yes at the top of her lungs, still floating from her encounter with Marion. But she remained calm when answering. "Yes, your salesman Marion was a great help," she said.

"There's no one that works here by that name," the lady replied with a puzzled look on her face.

"Are you sure?" Emma asked.

"Yes, I positive dear."

Emma fell silent. She paid for her things then exited the store with her uncle carrying her bags.

* * *

Charles propped his feet up on the supports as the young man began to dust the shoes with a brush. He applied a generous amount of polish making sure he got down in the seams as best as he could. Charles admired the kid's hustle and the attention to detail as he did his job.

"Where you from kid?" he asked sparking up conversation.

"I'm from the Bronx sir," the young kid replied.

"Yankee fan?" Charles asked.

"Yes sir," the kid said as a bright smile creased his face.

"Who's your favorite player?"

"Reggie Jackson," the kid said without any hesitation.

"Final Call, bean pies. Final Call, bean pies," a well-groomed brother called out as he came around the corner catching everyone's attention.

Charles could tell the brother was part of the Nation of Islam by the way he was dressed, black suit and a bowtie; and by the Final Call newspapers he held up in his hand.

"Final Call, my brother?" the man asked as he approached, seeing Charles relaxed getting his shoes shined. "This is the real news my black brother. Unbought and uncompromised."

"No thank you brother but you have a good day," Charles said in his normal cool and relaxed tone.

Still the man seemed to be offended. "You too busy doing the white man's work to open your mind up to the truth brother?" The man replied rudely.

"White man's work?" Charles questioned lowering his brow and sitting up in the chair.

"No disrespect 'cause I know who you are but you're out here dealing poison to your own kind. Killing your own community, doing the white man's job for him."

"Nigga please," Charles said. He had heard that one too many times for his liking from so called righteous guys like the man standing in front of him. "I know cats just like you, kicking all that black power, knowledge of self shit but they the biggest dope pushers in the neighborhood."

"Don't ever disrespect The Nation like that," the man said aggressively moving towards Charles only to be stopped by two of his bodyguards.

"Don't you ever disrespect me muthafucka," Charles retorted with authority. "Or I'll send you to Allah before you make your next Salah. Get this clown away from me," he instructed the men standing between them and they quickly led the man away.

Charles looked up seeing Emma emerge from one of the stores with a bag in her hand and his brother by her side carrying the rest of her bags. He shook his head and laughed. Emma had the same effect on all the men in her life. She could make them do anything she wanted them to. His smile quickly disappeared as he heard a clicking sound and felt the cold steel of handcuffs locking around his ankle.

"What the hell you doing?" He barked looking down at the young man shining his shoes. The kid never looked up at him. He just grabbed his shine box and sprinted around the corner. Charles tried to get up but couldn't, he was locked to the seat. The sound of tires screeching to a halt made him look towards the street. He watched helplessly as a group of men spilled from a cargo van with automatic weapons and began spraying the block. Locals scrambled down the street taking cover behind cars and slipping into stores like rats in their holes trying to avoid the hail of gunfire. Charles' men were not as lucky as bullets ripped through the unsuspecting men before they ever had a chance to reach for their guns. Charles pulled the gun from his waist and began firing at the men in the street.

The Muslim arguing with Charles's two bodyguards on the corner pulled a gun just as the men turned their attention to their boss. He fired a series of shots into both of their chests then ripped off his bow tie. He stepped over them and emptied the rest of the clip into them causing their bodies to jerk violently as each bullet hit.

* * *

Marion exited the store a few seconds behind Emma and watched as she walked up the block. As his eyes trailed her up the block some he noticed the commotion on the corner as a few guys in suits were arguing with a member of The Nation of Islam. The sound of a car skidding to a stop made his eyes shift to the street where a blue Chevy Nova had pulled behind a white cargo van. Marion watched as an Italian man emerged from the passenger side of the Nova wearing a long trench coat and sunglasses, the outline of a shotgun noticeable as he stepped onto the sidewalk.

"Oh shit," Marion thought to himself as the man pulled the sawed-off from his coat.

"Aaaaah!" Emma screamed at the top of her lungs as Gino pumped a shot into her uncle's Pee Wee's chest mistaking him for Charles. Blood splatter painted Emma's face from the blast and she began bawling uncontrollably.

"Emma!" Charles yelled as Gino snatched her by the arm. He tried to stand but caught a pair of bullets in his forearm and shoulder knocking him back into the chair.

"Daddy!" Emma cried out using every ounce of strength she had to wrestle away from Gino's powerful grip, but she was no match as he easily dragged her away towards the waiting Nova.

BANG! BANG! BANG!

Marion squeezed off a trio of shots hitting Gino square in the chest, killing him. As he fell dead to the ground he pulled Emma down with him. One of the men that leaped from the van turned to fire but Marion dropped him with a head shot causing the fake Muslim to flee up the block. Marion fired a few more shots sending bullets crashing through the back window of the Nova as it sped away following the white van.

"Daddy!" Emma screamed as she rose to her feet and

raced over to her father crying. Charles held his hand over his wound as blood seeped through his fingers. "Are you okay?" she asked in a panic.

"I'm fine," he lied through his clenched teeth, trying to keep Emma calm.

Marion raced over to Charles and Emma. "You okay?" he asked Charles seeing the blood from the wound in his shoulder.

"I'll be fine," Charles responded. "Where'd the hell you come from kid?" Charles jokingly asked. He was truly thankful the young stranger had been there.

"I just seen you needed help, so I helped," Marion answered.

"Thanks," Charles said.

"No problem," Marion replied. "How bout you, you alright?" he asked Emma. She was in pure shock, screaming and crying. He scanned her up and down checking to make sure she wasn't hit. She wasn't but she was shivering with fear. Marion quickly removed his shirt and wrapped it around her as she collapsed into his arms.

"Do me a favor," Charles asked. "Take this," he handed Marion his gun. "And get her outta here. She don't need to be here. I'll take care of all of this," he requested hearing all

the sirens in the distance getting closer and closer.

"Ok," Marion said.

Charles reached out and grabbed Marion by the arm. "I'm

trusting you with my most prized possession. Anything

happens to her, you're a dead man."

Marion nodded his understanding then lead a distraught

Emma away from the chaos.

Kingdom Come

CHAPTER 3

A few days later, a sharply dressed Marion stood at the bottom of the steps looking up at the double doors of the brownstone. Dozens of reporters, curious onlookers and police officers were crowding the front of the Matthews' home turning the somber affair into a spectacle.

"Have some respect," an annoyed Marion mumbled to himself as he pushed through the photographers and climbed the steps. He knocked on the door, after a few moments it opened up and a stoned faced, bull-necked man stepped out. Marion watched as the man carefully assessed him, then saw the recognition grow in his eyes. He was the young man that had saved the boss' life. Marion lifted his arms out to his side as the bodyguard patted him down then nodded with respect and stepped aside allowing him to enter the home. Inside the doorway two more brawny men were posted up. Guarding the door of the Matthews' home was an honor and neither seemed to be taking it lightly.

Marion suddenly felt out of place, like a whore in church as he moved into the living room past a slew of unfamiliar faces. An awkward silence covered the room and every eye seemed fixed on him. It was like everybody knew who he was but he didn't know a soul. He inhaled deeply and the sweet smell of flowers filled his nostrils, easing his nerves.

Charles' youngest brother Jimmy had been watching Marion since he entered the home. He didn't take to newcomers all that well and from the moment he had laid eyes on Marion, he didn't like him. He enjoyed watching Marion look out of place and hoped it made him feel uncomfortable. If it hadn't, he planned on doing his part to make him feel unwelcome. He decided to approach him after a few minutes of observing.

"You look lost my man," Jimmy said snapping his fingers

pretending not to know who Marion was. "All deliveries go through the back."

Marion ignored the sarcasm remaining cool and collected. "I'm here to see Charles," he replied.

"Damn, my brother just let anybody in his house," Jimmy quipped as he sized Marion up. "What, you collecting donations for the church? Let me see what I got for you," Jimmy said reaching in his pocket.

"Nah," Marion chuckled slightly. *This nigga a clown, he just missing the big red nose,* he thought to himself but stayed even. "I'm here about some business," he answered.

"Business?" Jimmy repeated with a bit of laughter. "What kind of business a nigga like you got with my brother?"

Marion's teeth clenched in anger. Fed up with Jimmy's shit and tired of playing games. "Nigga…" he began, unable to restrain his reaction before quickly catching himself.

At that moment Charles entered the room with his daughter close by his side. When Marion saw Emma he felt a rush of excitement but remained calm. She was even more stunning than he remembered. She moved with a grace that seemed effortless, her long legs gliding more than walking. The sadness in her eyes did nothing to dim her beauty. In fact, it added a softness to Emma that made her appear more relatable. She walked with her head up, displaying tons of courage, although her innocence had been ripped away. That impressed him the most. Marion had known many beautiful women but none captured his interest like Emma had. He wanted to know more about her. How she spent her time and most importantly, what made her smile. He decided right there that she would be his.

Emma greeted some of the guest with kisses on the cheeks, others she embraced with warm hugs as she walked around the room with her father. When they finally reached Marion Charles stuck out his hand to welcome him.

"Marion, I'm glad you could make it," he said as the men shook hands.

"How's that shoulder?" Marion asked seeing one of Charles's arms in a sling from where he had been shot the day the attempt was made on his life.

"Hurts like hell but I'm holding up," he replied. "They done tried six times, ain't got me yet," he bragged about the failed attempts to assassinate him.

"Oh, you're Marion," Jimmy chimed in with a false smile. "Why you ain't say that?"

"It's cool," Marion answered without ever looking in his direction.

"I see you already met my brother Jimmy," Charles said sensing a hint of tension between them. It was nothing new, he knew his brother tended to have that effect on people. Turning to the beautiful woman standing next to him, Charles proceeded to introduce her, "This is my sister-in-law, Pee Wee's wife."

"I'm sorry for your loss ma'am," Marion said shaking her hand. He had a way of making people feel comfortable and she looked pleased accepting his condolence.

"And you remember my daughter, Emma," Charles continued.

The sadness in Emma's eyes disappeared briefly. "I never got a chance to thank you for saving my life," she said holding onto his hand and staring into his brown eyes.

Marion felt honored by her words. "I'm sorry for your family's loss but I'm glad I was there to help."

Emma beamed, he had made her feel the same way she felt in the store the day they met. His words were polite but his look was confident. Tall, handsome and well dressed with a hint of mystery. Her physical attraction to him was immediate and undeniable, it was responsible for the pounding in her chest. Emma gazed at him intently as he caressed her hand, with every stroke she yearned to feel more.

Emma was snapped out of her brief mind trip as the group looked towards the door. An elderly Cuban gentleman dressed in a black suit and fedora came striding in.

Felix "The Cat" Santos aka El Gato was Charles Matthews connect. He was a man of portly presence that commanded the attention of everyone in the room. He took a puff of the lit cigar that hung from his mouth, blowing out a large cloud of smoke followed by a hacking cough. He removed his hat passing it to his son Andres, the handsome, dark-haired young man at his side. Felix immediately spotted the group and made his approach, his son following close behind. He gave Charles a look, receiving a slight nod in return, indicating the woman next to him was indeed his deceased brother's wife.

"My dear," Felix's thick Spanish accent poured out as he kissed her on both cheeks. "I so soddy we have to meet in des sad times," he said offering his condolences.

"Thank you," she said graciously.

"Emma, mi belleza," he said turning his jovial face as he

gawked at her as if he couldn't believe what he was seeing. He grabbed her by the hand spinning her around and gesturing to his son. "She gets more beautiful eddy time we see her, isn't that right?" Felix's large voice carried throughout the living room.

"Yes Papi," Andres responded watching his father fawn over Emma.

"Felix, my good friend," Charles greeted with a firm handshake. "Come this way," he pointed towards a door that led to his study. "We have a lot to talk about, I have somewhere we can speak in private." Felix and his son walked off followed by Jimmy. Charles turned back to Marion before walking away and said, "Stick around for a few kid, I wanna talk to you too."

Marion nodded but didn't say a word.

"Would you like something to eat?" Emma turned to Marion and offered. "The food is excellent."

"No, I'm okay. Thank you anyway."

Emma wasn't used to guys like Marion. Once most men laid their eyes on her they'd be falling all over themselves to get with her. But he wasn't most guys, she could see that and it intrigued her.

"Well at least let me show you around," she said.

"Why not," Marion replied as she grabbed him by the hand and led him away like a spirited child on a play date.

Marion admired the way Charles Matthews was living as they strode through the opulent brownstone and down a stairwell that spilled out to a small patch of grass in the back of the house.

"That was real cute, that little thing you pulled in the store," Emma smirked hiding her sarcasm. She had a natural sweetness about her that hid her true feelings and took the sting off her slick remarks."

"Sorry about that," Marion replied followed by charming grin.

"I bet that smile gets you out of all types of trouble, huh?"

Marion shrugged, "Or into it."

"I've thought about what happened every single day," Emma confessed as she walked ahead of him. "If we hadn't seen each other in the store or if you weren't there, what might have happened to me," she paused, the thought almost too much for her to handle.

"I don't waste time thinking about the what ifs and you shouldn't either. It will drive you crazy. It's better to enjoy the what is," he explained.

"Does it ever go away, the images?" she asked.

"With time," he said it more hoping for her sake, than knowing.

"Still, I think it was fate how we met," she said. Emma knew he was trailing closely behind. She could feel his body moving in stride with hers.

Marion stopped walking and stared at Emma, "Maybe. I'm just glad I was there."

Feeling she was now walking alone Emma turned around to face him. Marion stood with his hands in his pockets. He had to be the most handsome man she had ever laid eyes on. Her physical attraction was obvious but she felt a deeper connection. "Me too," Emma responded.

Marion extended his hand summoning for her to get close to him. Emma instinctively reached for his touch without hesitation. Standing in her backyard Marion didn't seem like an outsider, for some reason she felt like he belonged. Her father kept her sheltered from outsiders, mainly for her protection but he also preached that most people weren't worthy to be in her presence. Being near Marion felt right, it felt necessary. Marion pulled her close to him, when he spoke the tiny hairs on the nape of her neck stood up firmly.

"I believe everything happens for a reason," Marion stated.

"Even my uncle's death?" Emma asked sadly, her eyes falling from his.

"As bad as it may sound. Yeah, even his death," he said.

"Why do you speak like that?" she questioned.

"Like what?" He replied.

"Like nothing phases you. Like you're so much older and more experienced. So serious. You're not like most guys my age," she explained.

Marion smiled, "I've seen things most people twice my age haven't."

Emma stepped closer to him. Their faces were only inches apart. "So what do you see now," she flirted.

Marion cupped her chin so she could see the sincerity in his eyes and feel the truth in his words. He couldn't understand why but the connection he felt to Emma was one that he needed to explore even though he knew the dangers it could lead to. Charles Matthews was a very powerful man and although Marion didn't fear a soul, he still knew he had to play it smart. Still he wanted her, he felt she needed his protection. He needed to be in her life.

"I see that you're sheltered," he told her. "I see that you're loved by your family. I see the way they protect you. But I know you want to experience life outside of your home, I can see the desire in your eyes. I know you're nervous right now by the way your hands are all clammy."

Emma pulled her hands away in embarrassment but Marion grabbed them back reassuring her it was okay. "I know you like me, I could tell by the way you lit up when you saw me in your home today." He said.

"Well you did save my life," Emma tried her best to justify her actions.

"It's ok," his bright smile melted any fight she tried to put up. "Seeing that confirms that I am supposed to be right here. So maybe you're right. Maybe it was fate."

Emma couldn't help but to admire him. It felt like the Fourth of July in her stomach, with every word he said the biggest and prettiest fireworks would go off.

"You're the most beautiful woman I've ever laid eyes on."

Emma was caught in the moment, wrapped in his words and her emotions. She closed her eyes and pushed up on her tiptoes to kiss him. But no kiss came back, she opened her eyes to see Marion staring her in the face. She was embarrassed but Marion quickly made that feeling disappear.

"I'm guessing you think I'm beautiful too huh?" He joked. Then pointed to his eyes indicating he thought somebody could be watching.

Emma played along, burying her head in his chest and they shared a laugh before heading back into the house.

* * *

Andres Santos stood unseen, watching from the study window as Marion and Emma talked in the backyard sharing a couple of laughs. When they finally disappeared into the house he walked over and took a seat next to his father.

Charles was leaning up against the front of the desk, he popped a painkiller in his mouth and sipped from a glass of water to wash it down. He rubbed his good hand over his head as he did his best to explain what exactly happened the day his brother was killed.

"As much as it makes me sad, de loss of ju brudda puts a major question mark on our business relationship moving forward," Felix interrupted speaking in choppy English.

"What kind of question mark?" Charles quizzed.

"What my father is trying to say," the younger Santos intervened. He spoke smoothly but with a brazen assurance. "The way your brother was gunned down. The fact that somebody had the balls to try something like that in your own neighborhood. Makes us question if you are losing power," he said coldly. "If that's the case and your power has slipped some, it's only a matter of time before your enemies invade your territory. That would mean war. When there is war, no money is being made, which is never good for business."

Charles stared at Andres Santos with a fiery calm. He didn't appreciate the tone or boldness he spoke with. Andres hadn't earned the right to even speak with someone of Charles status and until now he never had. The only thing keeping Charles from wrapping his hands around his neck was the respect he had for Felix.

"Si, Si," Felix nodded in agreement with his son between coughs. "I've seen my share of war in my lifetime," he shook his head back and forth. "No good. Even when ju win, sometimes ju lose."

"I can guarantee you that is not the case," Charles said. "But I can show you better than I can tell you. Anybody crazy enough to attack me, I will personally show them the end of the world."

Charles was thought of as a shrewd businessman but he was far more ruthless than he was giving credit for. He planned on making whoever was responsible pay dearly. Charles handed Felix a copy of the daily newspaper. On the front page was a picture of a young man's dead body stuffed in a leather trunk along with a pair of freshly shined shoes. The trunk had been pulled from the Harlem River.

"I love dis' guy," Felix bellowed looking at his son while pointing at Charles then letting out a hearty laugh.

Andres handed the fedora to his father then rose to his feet. "We have to go Papi."

Placing the hat on his head as he stood up, Felix put the cigar back into his mouth then shook Charles hand firmly. "Excuse my son, his mouth earlier," Felix explained. "He hasn't learned how to say things de right way, ju understand right? One day dis will all be his to run. I'm getting too old for all dis stuff but he still has a long way to go," Felix informed Charles.

Charles smirked, "I understand." He extended his hand to the younger Santos. "Congrats, I always wish for a son of my own to pass all this down to," Charles revealed.

Andres shook Charles hand. "You got a month to show us your control of Harlem hasn't slipped or we'll take our business somewhere else," he said before he and his father exited the room.

Charles walked over to the window and noticed that evening was slowly setting in. The house had quieted down some and he could tell that some of the guest had begun to clear out. He stared at his reflection in the window. His thoughts were scattered still trying to wrap his mind around Pee Wee's death and The Santos' ultimatum. In the window glass he saw the mental stress all over his face. He took a deep breath, closed his eyes trying to empty the thoughts in his mind and quite the rage of his pounding heart. After a few moments, Charles regained his composure. By the time Marion knocked on the door he was calm and felt like himself again. "Come in," he said.

Marion pushed open the door and stuck his head into the room. "One of your guys out there said you were ready to talk," he said stepping inside the room.

"Yeah, close the door behind you," Charles said stepping away from the window and pointing to a chair in front of the desk. "Have a seat," he said taking his place in the chair behind the desk. "I wanted to speak with you alone for a second. Let me ask you a question? Where'd you learn to handle a gun like that?"

"U.S Army," a relaxed Marion answered.

"My brother Pee Wee was an army man," Charles replied then paused, rubbing his hand over his chin as if he was carefully choosing his next statement. "I could really use someone with your set of skills in my organization. What do you think about coming to work for me?"

Marion remained silent for a moment, composed and emotionless, almost unimpressed by the offer. "I've been in the Army for the past four years. And I don't mean any disrespect but I'm kinda done being a foot soldier, if you know what I mean," he said. "But if you're offering something more than I'm all ears," Marion finished his statement with a smile.

Charles really liked the young man sitting in front of him. He had the guts of a burglar and exuded a poise beyond his years. Charles thought he showed great potential. He stood and put his hand on Marion's shoulder. "Normally when I offer someone a job within my organization they have a much different reaction," Charles laughed, getting a kick out of Marion's calm demeanor. He shook his head as he crossed the room staring out the window again. "Something more like what?" Charles asked.

"I got a small crew of my own out in Brooklyn. A few solid guys I trust. With the right connect and a steady flow of some quality dope, I know I can be much more of an asset to you than just some hired gun," he proposed.

"You're sharp," Charles acknowledged.

"You mind if I ask what that thing the other day was about?" Marion questioned.

"The Martello family has been trying to muscle in on my business lately. They're not getting a piece of the action and they're not happy about it. They tried to snatch my daughter to force me to negotiate. They think she's my weakness," he said seemingly out of the blue.

"Is she?" Marion asked.

"My wife died when Emma was young. I've raised her by myself, along with help from my brothers but mostly by myself. Everything I do is for her, she is more of a source of strength than a weakness. Joseph Martello wants a piece of everything I've built; which means he's not only trying to take from me but from her too. I'll never let that happen. You understand?" Charles turned and faced him just as Marion nodded his head.

Part of Marion couldn't understand why a man he barely knew had opened up to him so personally. But the other part of him appreciated Charles' position and respected him for the amount of love he displayed for his daughter. Not to mention the strength he showed as leader of their family.

"Dig this," Charles spoke up like a light had gone on in his head. "I got a little job I need taken care of. I got a tip that the fake Muslim motherfucker is hiding out in Brooklyn. I know that's your stomping grounds. I need you to find him and bring him to me. You think you can handle that?"

"No problem," Marion replied.

"You do that and you got a deal." Charles said.

Marion knew this was the opportunity he had been waiting for. He wasn't about to let it slip through his fingers. He needed the help of somebody that knew what they were doing and he had the perfect person in mind. Someone he trusted with his life.

Kingdom Come

CHAPTER 4

Emma sat in her bedroom staring through the window, she watched as her father and Marion exited her brownstone. When they reached the curb, the two of them shook hands before going their separate ways.

Emma caressed and twisted the ends of her long flowing hair as it rested on her shoulder, something she did when she got nervous. She did it in an absent minded manner, not realizing what she was doing. Emma continued to stare out the window but her mind was fixated on Marion. She couldn't get pass the connection she felt with him.

She had crushes before, but never like this. There was something special about Marion that shook her soul and she urgently needed to explore that feeling until she understood why.

"What got you all googly eyed?" Ms. Tina asked as she walked into the bedroom holding freshly washed and folded sheets for Emma's bed.

Ms. Tina was the closest thing Emma had to a mother figure. She was the housekeeper but more importantly, she was the only women Emma felt comfortable speaking with. Her father did his best and was very active in her life but when it came to things that only a woman could handle, Ms. Tina stepped in; especially when it came to matters of the heart. Being constantly surrounded by nothing but men, Emma sincerely appreciated Ms. Tina's presence and valued her opinion.

"Nothing" Emma responded with a slight giggle.

"Uh huh," Ms. Tina replied. "Well, whatever Mr. Nothing's name is, he's really handsome," she teased. "I saw the two of you out back," she informed Emma, setting the sheets down on the bed. "I saw how you lit up around him too," she nodded her head before continuing. "And I saw how he looks at you. I remember that look. My Louis once looked at me like that," she reminisced. "I looked at him the exact same way you staring out that window at Mr. Nothing out there."

Emma tried to hide her excitement but she couldn't deny what Ms. Tina was saying. That was exactly what she wanted to hear. She wanted to know that how she was feeling was okay, someone else could see the same thing just by looking at them together. Emma got up from the bench by her window and walked over to her bed and sat down.

"Well Ms. Tina," Emma cooed, "You might be right. That young man is something special, he saved my life you know? I feel like it's meant to be for us."

"Emma, you know I love you like I birthed you myself," Ms. Tina spoke in a warm loving tone. "And you may think that I'm just boring old Ms. Tina that keeps to herself and doesn't meddle in anything. But one thing you need to know baby, is that I have been you before. Trust me, as much as I love you, cleaning up and keeping house after you and your father was not what I had planned for my life," she said honestly. "I know what it is to be in love with a man and most of all to be in love with a man in power. I see the potential in that young man out there, he has the same spark in his eye that your daddy had at that age," she revealed as Emma played close attention to every word. "Now what I need you to understand is that you're in a privileged position. You get to reap all the beautiful benefits of being the most respected man in Harlem's daughter. Your daddy makes sure you want for nothing and he keeps you sheltered from what your ears and eyes don't need to experience. But being the daughter of a boss and being the woman on the arm of a boss is a whole different ball game. You hear and see everything. You are him and he is you. When his back is up against the wall and the ceilings start to cave in that same man who protects you and loves you, is gonna need you to do the same for him, in more ways than one. It may come a time that he needs you to get on the stand and be his alibi or pull the trigger with precision without hesitation. You have to ask yourself Emma, are you ready for that? Is that even what you want? Or better yet, can you love him enough to be willing to do all of that?"

Emma sat silent, her mind filled with so many thoughts as Ms. Tina spoke.

"See a King is nothing without a Queen. But a Queen silently runs the castle while her King gets all the praise. Can you deal with that? It is a hard job. When you choose this lifestyle Emma, everything ain't all bad…but it definitely ain't all good."

"I've been around this my whole life Ms. Tina, this is all I know," Emma tried explaining. "Plus Marion is different. I can feel his soul connect with mine. I saw how my mommy was with my daddy. She loved every inch of him. On her saddest day, he was the only one who could make her smile. The small amount of years I had with her, I remembered that the most. I remember her eyes only twinkled when he walked in the room and her smile grew the brightest when he kissed her forehead. I want that for myself," she confessed. "I feel like smiling that big when I see or think about Marion." Emma knew what Ms. Tina was saying was true but her heart couldn't let her accept it fully. She knew it would be consequences but she didn't care. She didn't know if she felt so strongly about Marion because he saved her life or because she felt fate had brought her a soul mate. But one thing was certain, she never felt like this before. She had to at least give it a chance, explore the feelings she was having. Emma was iron willed and strong-minded. She wouldn't allow anything or anyone to get in the way of what she wanted.

"I was there too," Ms. Tina reminded her. "Don't you forget now. I was there to see your mother smile when your father walked in the room. I saw that same twinkle that you speak of. But I was also there to wipe the mascara that ran down her cheek when she cried herself to sleep because that same man made her cry from fear he would be killed. Your mom and I were good friends before I worked here and one of your daddy's closest partners was once the love of my life," she paused as her face grew sad from the thought of lost love. "Your momma and I had big dreams, we were gonna be Queens of the city. Your daddy and my Louis were gonna be the sho'nuff Kings," Ms. Tina shook her head. But life ain't like the fairy tales, reality will bite you in the ass and slap you in the face."

Emma's face held a look of shock, she had no idea about Ms. Tina's history with her family. Ms. Tina was more than meets the eye and now Emma understood why she always had jewels to give her.

"I know you got your mind made up already baby girl. I can see it in your eyes. Shoot, I knew your mind was made up before I even opened my mouth," Ms. Tina let out a chuckle. "Just know if you ever need me, I am here." Ms.

Tina picked up the empty basket that had held the sheets and headed for the door.

"Ms. Tina," Emma called out.

"Yes baby," she turned and answered.

"What ever happened to Louis? Did he go to jail?" Emma asked interested in knowing but also showing her naiveté of her youth.

"No baby, he didn't. They killed my Louis, right on Broadway, the day I was going to tell him I was pregnant with our first child."

Emma's face saddened and her heart skipped a beat when she heard Ms. Tina's reply. "But…you don't have any kids," she spoke in a confused whisper.

"I know. Like I said Emma, life ain't like the fairy tales. It's not always a happy ending."

* * *

"Look at this black muthafucka here," Marion called out with excitement from a back table in Nelle's bar. The place had yet to open for the day and his voice echoed throughout the empty place.

"Ay, you block headed son of a bitch," the man yelled

back in a thick southern accent as the two closed the distance between them and hugged like long lost brothers.

"Nate the Skate," Marion said to his old army buddy.

Nate Walker had never been up North before, until he joined the army, he had barely ventured outside of his hometown of Shreveport, Louisiana. He was country and proud of it. He talked plenty of shit and backed it all up. He and Marion had become fast friends and eventually grew tight as brothers while over in Vietnam. Nate was the one person Marion trusted more than anybody in the world.

"Got damn me," Nate said looking at his well dress buddy. "You clean as a clap doctor, you son of a bitch."

Marion laughed. "This the country nigga I been telling you about," he said turning to Goose, who was standing just behind him. "This is Nate. He's like my brother. The S.O.B had my back the whole time while we were in 'Nam."

"Muthafuckin' right," Nate said.

Goose stuck out his hand. "Marion says you his family, then you my family."

"Ok then family," Nate said shaking Goose's hand. "You got anything strong enough to knock the hair off a wolf's pussy behind that bar?" he asked causing the group to burst into laughter.

The men walked over to the bar, Marion and Nate took a seat as Goose went behind the bar and grabbed a bottle of cognac and a few glasses. He poured the group some shots as the two friends caught up.

"You look like you doing pretty good fo' yo'self up here," Nate said. "If a man can make it up here, he can make it anywhere. Ain't that right?"

"Shit, we bout to be doing a whole lot better, now that you're here," Marion said with confidence. "I gotta lil' job for us. We pull it off," he paused letting his words trail off. "And the world is our oyster."

Nate tossed back a shot of liquor and slammed the glass back onto the bar. "Shit, who I gotta kill." He was pure gangster. If he wanted something you possessed, he took it. If you opposed, he killed you. It was that simple with him. And he was unwavering in his loyalty to Marion.

"My nigga," Marion said and gulped his shot.

CHAPTER 5

Inside a rundown apartment in Bushwick, Harold sat on the edge of the bed in a cold sweat with a lit cigarette in his trembling hand. His nerves and his jones were getting the best of him. He had gotten word that Charles Matthews was looking for him and he knew that meant the Italians he had done the hit with were looking for him too. He was a loose end, he knew they would kill him just to keep him from telling Charles who was behind the hit. The long ash at the tip of his cigarette looked as if it would fall at any moment. He took two long drags then snuffed it out in the ashtray and began getting dressed. He put on his pants in a rush and rose to his feet. The bed he had just rolled out of felt like a board and he stretched his arms to the sky trying to loosen up his stiff back. He frantically searched for his shoes amongst the clutter of trash that cover the floor. Once he located them, he slid them on his feet and slipped his shirt over his head. The noise caused the naked woman in the bed to stir. She rolled over sitting up in the bed and clicked on the lamp. She watched for a second as he paced the room then walked over and peeked through the curtains as he mumbled to himself.

"Where you think you going?" she sassed.

"Bitch, who you questioning," he shouted cocking back his hand as she coward to avoid being slapped. Harold chuckled at the sight of her fear. "Since you need to know so muthafuckin' bad, I'm going to score some dope bitch," he informed her. He had been held up in the house with her for a couple days and the monkey on his back had grown into a gorilla. He was dripping with sweat and scratching his arm in need of a fix.

"Don't call me a bitch again," she shot back.

"Or what?" he barked while charging at her, grabbing her by the hair and dragging her out the bed as she screamed.

"Or I'll cut your fucking throat," she yelled as she pressed the tip of a switch blade to his throat.

Harold hadn't notice her pull the weapon from under the pillow and he froze; caught off guard once he felt the pinch of the blade's tip in his neck. "Hey hold on now sweet thang," he tried negotiating with his hands to the side. "I was only jiving with you. I didn't mean nothing by it." Feeling her relax some, Harold suddenly grabbed her wrist twisting it backwards until the knife fell from her hands, then backhanded her back onto the bed. "Bitch, you must have lost your goddamn mind!" He picked up the knife and pinned her to the bed by the throat. Harold pressed the sharp blade against the side of her face, "I should cut your pretty little face up into a million pieces," he threatened as she sobbed and tears rolled down her face. Harold leaped to his feet and closed the knife, slipping it into his pocket. He snatched her purse off the dresser and took the cash out then grabbed his jacket that hung on the back of the door before heading for the stairs.

Out on the street, Marion settled into the front seat of the car as a light rain dotted the windshield. At that time of night, the strip on Bushwick Avenue was pretty quiet except for the junkies that staggered up the block every now and then. It hadn't been as hard to find Harold as Marion originally thought. Once he got the word Harold had a fondness for heroin and prostitutes, Marion knew there was only a matter of time before his addiction caused him to slip up. Word quickly got back that Harold was laying up with a yellow bone whore named Tweety in an apartment on Bushwick Avenue.

Marion watched a light go on inside the apartment over the barbershop and saw a figure moving back and forth. A sliver of light came through the curtains as they opened slightly and Harold peered out the window.

"There go that muthafucka right there," Marion said spotting him in the window. Nate looked up just as Harold ducked back in the curtains. "Be ready," Marion instructed.

Nate's eyes were shifty, gazing coldly at his surroundings in search of something to harm. He got off on committing murder. Killing gave him a hard on. He got an excitement from taking a person's life that nothing else could match, not even sex.

Marion slipped his gun into his coat. He pulled his hat down over his head and stepped out the car as Nate pulled off. Hustling across the street, Marion ducked into an adjacent alley just as Harold walked out the front of the building.

Harold pulled his jacket closed as he hurried up the block and cut through the alley. He passed right by Marion never seeing him tucked in the shadows leaning against the wall. His thoughts solely on finding some dope to score. He was starting to hurt bad and needed his medicine.

Marion emerged from the darkness and began following an unsuspecting Harold down the alley. He pulled the gun from his coat, letting it fall to his side as he continued to shadow his target.

Harold slowed his pace some, seeing a car up ahead in the alley with its brake lights on and hazards flashing. The closer he got he could see a man bent over in the trunk searching for something. When the man looked up and spotted Harold, he flagged him down and asked for help.

"Hey my man, could you give me a hand getting this tire outta here? I caught a flat," the man called out.

Harold sighed a deep breath as he walked towards the man. He really needed to score but he figured he'd help out quickly, maybe get some cash for his troubles and be on his way.

"Thanks," the man said as Harold approached. "I can't seem to get the damn spare tire out."

"Watch out let me see if I can get it," Harold said sticking his head inside the trunk. To his surprise there was no tire to be found. "Ah, ain't no tire in here m—" then he felt a thud to the back of his head as Marion hit him with the gun and things went black.

Marion and Nate lifted Harold's unconscious body into the trunk and slammed it close.

* * *

Charles Matthews took a swig from his flask and felt the burn of the cognac inside his chest. Finally, he would have his revenge. He had been shot twice, one of the bullets entering right above his heart. Even now, the slug was still lodged in his shoulder and ached every time he moved. He lifted the sling over his head grunting loudly as he removed it. He started opening and closing his fist, trying to work out the pain and regain some of the feeling in his arm. His eyes grew dark and cold as his rage simmered inwardly threatening to boil over at any moment. The amount of pain and torture he planned on inflicting on the man responsible for murdering his brother played over and over in his mind.

Charles looked out of the office where his brothers were

congregating and saw a burgundy Buick backing into the warehouse. Adrenaline began to pump through his body numbing his pain as his heart raced and his muscles twitched and tensed up. He walked out into the warehouse. At that moment, the doors on the Buick opened and Marion and Nate appeared.

Marion looked around at the dim and damp warehouse with all concrete floors and walls. There were no windows and no fresh air flowing through the place. It reminded him of a tomb and he could tell Charles had killed his share of men there.

"Mr. Matthews," Marion said extending his hand and Charles shook it firmly. "This is Nate Walker," he said introducing his right hand man.

"Where is he?" Charles asked almost rudely but unintentionally not speaking to Nate as his anxiousness got the best of him.

Nate tossed Marion the keys then walked to the back of the car and popped the trunk.

When Harold saw Charles staring down at him, his eyes nearly popped out of his head from shock and fear. He immediately began to beg for his life. Marion dragged him from the trunk effortlessly and tossed him at Charles's feet.

"I held up my end," Marion reminded him. "So do we have a deal?"

"Hell yeah," Charles replied. "But stick around, I want you to see this." Suddenly, all of Charles's well thought out plans of torture instantly were forgotten. A murderous rage took over him as he attacked Harold with the utmost savagery. Kicking and beating him repeatedly. Charles foamed out the corners of his mouth like a rabid animal delivering blow after blow. Before long he was breathing heavily and sweating profusely through his dress shirt. He stepped back to catch his breath, unbuttoning his shirt removing it to reveal his white tank top and muscular frame. His stout build and thick overhanging brow made him look like a vicious bulldog.

The rest of the Matthews brothers began circling around Harold like sharks when they smell blood in the water. They each took their turns pummeling him then tore at his clothes as Charles gave the order to strip Harold naked.

The brothers dragged Harold's battered body over to a large piece of plastic tarp that covered a section of the warehouse floor, it was surely the place they plan for him to die. There was nothing but darkness in Charles' eyes as he stood over Harold. He wanted his death to be long and drawn out.

He pulled the gun from his waist and fired. The first bullet entered Harold's right kneecap, the next entered his left. Two more bullets followed into each of his elbows. Harold let out agonizing screams as more slugs ripped through both ankles and shoulders. Harold writhed on the floor without any sense of control of his body as he tried to deal with the pain. Charles wanted him to suffer, he knew that was the only way he could get him to talk and tell him everything he wanted to know.

Silently, Charles turned and walked away. The cries of his victim playing like jazz in his ears seemed to bring a calm to his fury, if only momentarily. He stood between Marion and Nate reloading his gun. Both men knew he was trying to send them a message. It was why he wanted them to stay around and witness his brutality, in case they ever thought of crossing him in the future.

"See you gotta let the pain soak in," Charles explained. "Let those bullet wounds swell up some. It softens 'em up." His eyes twinkled with joy and his mouth twisted into a sadistic smirk, he walked back over to a bloodied Harold.

"Who hired you?" he snarled. When he received no answer, Charles took aim at Harold's crotch and pulled the trigger. Every man in the room turned their head to avoid seeing Harold's genitals explode into mush. A loud wailing cry swept over the warehouse as the walls threw back the echoes of Harold's pleas for mercy. "I think he's ready to talk now," Charles shouted looking around the room. He leaned in, getting as close to his victim as possible then questioned him once again, his teeth clenched in anger. "I said, who hired you?"

Kingdom Come

CHAPTER 6

Marion's business savvy was limitless and his leadership skills were unmatched. He was on top of the world. Within three months time his plan had come together. With the coke and heroin he was getting from Charles Matthews, he had taken over his Brooklyn neighborhood and was establishing a lucrative drug organization. His emergence as a leader in the drug game had not gone unnoticed by some of the power players in the city. Mainly the mob; who had begun to hear rumblings about the money being made in and around Williamsburg. Despite that, Marion was able to avoid any setbacks and thwart any attempt to deprive him of controlling the neighborhood. The streets had nothing but respect for Marion.

One morning he and Nate sat waiting for Goose to return with a shipment, some bricks of cocaine and a couple of kilos of heroin. The run was taking Goose longer than usual and Marion had a gut feeling something wasn't right. He continually switched up the routes to make sure his crew avoided not only the guys looking to rob them but the police as well. Lost shipments meant lost money and police contact of any kind was never good for business. He didn't need one of his young guys getting jammed up and folding under the pressure. His obsessive attention to detail, along with a consistent flow of cash had earned him a great deal of favor with Charles Matthews. But it made a few people jealous of his rise to power, Jimmy, Charles' youngest brother being one of them.

Marion's suspicions were confirmed as soon as Goose and Sonny walked through the door. Goose held a bloody towel over a gash on his head and the front of his shirt was blood stained as well. He appeared to be dazed and unstable as Sonny assisted him. Marion and Nate leaped from their seats and rushed over to help. They led Goose over to a seat and Marion immediately started to grill Sonny.

"What the fuck happened to him?" the seriousness in his tone evident.

"I-I don't know. We—" Sonny's voice cracked slightly as Marion pressed him for answers.

"Man, we got robbed," Goose finished his sentence as he grimaced.

"What!" Marion barked.

"Yeah, it's like they came out of nowhere," Sonny said. He was clearly shaken up. All that tough guy attitude of his had vanished.

"Tell me exactly what happened?" Marion demanded.

"Man some niggas got the drop on us. We made the transaction with Jimmy, like usual. We pull out, get a few blocks away and niggas box us in. They hopped out with guns drawn and took the load," Goose explained. "It was like they knew the route."

Marion remained silent but everyone in the room could

see the wheels in his head turning. He looked away from both
Goose and Sonny then over at Nate. He immediately knew
who had something to do with the stolen shipment. "Jimmy
is behind this shit, I know it." he said.

Jimmy had been against his brother doing business with
Marion from the beginning. He had been throwing shit in the
game and now this. The shipment going missing put Marion
in a bind, Charles had fronted it to him on consignment. He
had to get the money or the dope or shit could get ugly quick.

Goose shook his head, "I can't see it. Why would Jimmy
steal from us?" he asked. "Stealing from us is really stealing
from his brother. Why the fuck would he do that?"

"Never put all your trust in only what your eyes can see,"
Marion schooled him. "It's the things you can't see that are
the most dangerous."

"I gotta use the bathroom," Sonny said holding his
stomach. His nerves were getting the best of him and he had
the bubble guts. He hadn't stopped moving since they came
in the door.

Before he could leave, Marion called out to him.
"Sonny."

The young man stopped in his tracks and turned to face

him, "Yeah, what's up?"

"Don't be gone too long," Marion said, his face showed no emotion.

Sonny huffed and puffed then let out a sarcastic chuckle.

"They done scared the shit out of that boy, literally," Nate joked as Sonny quickly walked away and everybody laughed.

Marion wasn't satisfied, he needed more answers, "The thing that gets me is how he figure out the route?" Marion rubbed his chin and took a seat sighing deeply. "Did you follow the routine to make sure you didn't pick up a tail?"

"Yeah. We did all that, twists, turns, spun the block and everything. We weren't being followed," Goose declared. "I'm telling you cuz, it's like they came out of nowhere."

"They had to know the route," Nate said.

"You the only person I told," Marion said staring directly at Goose. They had been friends for a very long time. Marion never knew him to be anything except trustworthy but money had a way of bringing things out of people that you didn't know was there.

"What the fuck you trying to say?" Goose asked. His chest swelled with air and he sat up in his seat. He felt uncomfortable under Marion's glare. "You got something on your mind, come wit' it. We been friends too long to beat around the bush."

Nate's gaze grew frigid. His eyes were so dark, staring at him was like looking into a black hole. All it took was for Marion to give the nod and he would put a hole in Goose's head.

"Everybody cool out," Marion instructed feeling the tension build in the room. "Let's backtrack a bit. Tell me how the day went," he said.

Goose removed the bloody towel from his head before speaking. "Nothing special, I got up, got dressed, Sonny knocked on the door this morning, I let him in. Then you called and told me the route. The only person I told was…" Goose paused before he continued. "…was Sonny," he revealed slowly as his eyebrows rose with a hint of suspicion.

Marion had always had his reservations about Sonny but Goose had vouched for him so he let it ride. "Sonny," Marion repeated nodding his head. "Was there ever a time you left him alone today?"

"Yeah," Goose began. "I was running late this morning. Didn't eat anything, so I stopped at the corner store to get a buttered roll and a coffee before we drove out. I left Sonny alone in the car."

"He could have used the pay phone to alert Jimmy," Nate whispered to Marion who was already thinking the same thing.

"Go get him," Marion told Nate, who pulled out his gun and walked towards the bathroom.

"Why would Sonny be working with Jimmy though?" Goose asked confused.

"Jealousy and greed are a helluva combination," Marion explained.

"Muthafucka," Nate shouted, emerging from the bathroom. His outburst grabbed everyone's attention. "That nigga gone," he barked. "He climbed out the window."

"Guilty as charged," Marion replied looking back at Goose.

"He made a mistake Marion," Goose said in a somber tone. "We know it, and he knows it. He's probably just afraid. Let me talk to him and find out what's really going on," he pleaded with Marion.

"Ain't shit to talk about," Nate spat. "He stole from us."

"He's just a kid," Goose sympathized. "Let me talk some sense into him."

"He's playing a grown man's game," Marion said with a deathly calm to his voice.

"A deadly game," Nate piled on.

"You getting soft on me, Goose?" Marion asked. "Maybe this ain't your thing no more, I can understand. You got a wife now, a legit business with the bar. Maybe all this is out of your system."

Goose knew there was no sense in trying to plead any further, Marion had already decided Sonny's fate. No mercy or sympathy would be given. Any more protest and he would look guilty too and he wasn't, so Sonny was on his own.

"I say we kill that muthafucka Jimmy too," Nate exclaimed.

"Can't kill Jimmy without going to war with Charles," Marion told the both of them.

"Jimmy don't give a fuck about his own brother, he basically stole from him too. We'd be doing Charles a favor." Nate said.

"I don't think he'd see it quite like you do Skate," Goose laughed.

"He stole the shipment hoping his brother would blame us. Thinking we was trying to pull a fast one. At the very least he's thinking it will make Charles cut off our supply, maybe even worse," Marion explained. "Regardless, Jimmy is the connects brother, we can't kill him without going to war with Charles. Sonny is another story though. He means nothing to Charles. Killing him will also send a message to Jimmy, that we're on to his bullshit."

Nate and Goose nodded in agreement.

"You want me to take care of it," Nate asked, eager for the chance to maim something.

"Nah Skate, I'm gonna take care of this one personally," Marion said.

CHAPTER 7

It was a little after two in the morning when Sonny woke up shivering. His eyes were still heavy as he opened them and sat up in bed. Despite the thick comforter on the bed, he was freezing. *Why the hell is it so cold in here?* he thought to himself. Sonny gave his eyes time to adjust to the darkness before scanning the room. The spot on the bed next to him was empty, though the covers had been pulled back and there were several pillows lying there. Sonny was on the run and his nerves were fried. He had been convinced by Jimmy to betray Marion for five thousand dollars. He now realized it wasn't worth it. Anybody thinking of crossing Marion had to think twice because he would send Nate after them. Nate enjoyed the hunt, it made him feel like he was back in Vietnam. Having him looking for you was the most unsettling feeling in the world. Had he had more brains, Sonny would have known better.

Sonny continued to scan the room. Everything was just like he remembered before falling asleep. Nothing had been disturbed, except for the bedroom window, it was slightly cracked. He remembered closing the window before going to bed, only one person could have reopened it.

"This bitch keeps it freezin' in this muthafucka. I told her ass about this fuckin' window," he growled as he got up out of bed. The apartment belonged to the young lady he spoke of but he behaved like it was his.

He walked over to the window and peeked through it. A fire-escape led down to a dark alley. Sonny could see the swirling winds outside the window and could feel the temperature had dropped in the past couple of hours. He noticed something else too, footprints. He looked again at the alleyway below. He didn't see anyone or anything moving below. Sonny examined the steps of the fire-escape, above the window, more footprints. They were all different sizes. Sonny shrugged his shoulders assuming that they had to belong to some neighborhood kids. He chalked his suspicion up to the anxiety he felt from hiding out. He slammed the window shut and walked back to the bed, quickly getting underneath the thick comforter again. In just a matter of minutes he was asleep again.

Marion stood still and silent inside the closet watching Sonny's every move. He waited until he heard him snoring before exiting the closet. Marion wore a black beanie on his head, all black clothes and black leather gloves on his hands. He removed a blade from the inner pocket of his jacket. Moving like a cat burglar, he approached the side of the bed. Sonny was lying on his stomach snoring loudly, the back of his neck exposed. Marion positioned the tip of the blade a few inches from Sonny's neck. Then he grabbed him by the hair and swiftly plunged the blade into the back of Sonny's neck. He thrusted the knife in with such force that the jagged tip reappeared soaked with blood through the other side of Sonny's throat. Sonny's eyes popped open as blood oozed from his mouth. His entire body began to shake violently. He tried to bring his hands up to his throat but found himself unable to move. Marion twisted the knife and Sonny suddenly stopped shaking. Lying motionless on the bed his eyes remained open, but they were empty of any life. Marion removed the blade and wiped it on the comforter. Blood began slowly soaking the bed sheets as a crimson circle formed around Sonny.

At that moment, Marion was startled by a noise inside the bedroom. His eyes darted up and standing across the room was a beautiful girl in her early 20's. Her skin was coffee brown and her hair was pulled into a ponytail. She was wearing a robe and nothing else. The front was completely untied and exposed her perky breasts, shapely figure and landing strip styled vagina. When her eyes met Marion's, out of fear she dropped the sandwich she was holding in her hand. She opened her mouth to scream but before she could let out a sound, Marion pulled a gun from his waistband. He snatched a pillow from off the bed, placing it in front of the gun then squeezed the trigger. The room lit up with a flash as the pillow muffled the sound of the shot. The girl fell dead to the floor. There was a hole in the front of her head and blood was running down her face.

"Sorry baby girl, no witnesses," Marion said as he

Ty Marshall
stepped over her body, then vanished through the window.

CHAPTER 8

Jimmy stormed into the room Charles used as an office like a bat out of hell. His fury was obvious as he walked over to Charles and handed him the newspaper.

Charles unfolded it and read the headline about two bodies found in a small Brooklyn apartment. Then turned to Jimmy and asked, "Is this supposed to mean something to me?"

"That's the kid, Sonny," Jimmy said. "He works for Marion. I'm willing to bet Marion was behind this. Killing his own guy to cover up for the missing shipment." Jimmy had been trying for days to convince his brother that Marion had staged the robbery in order to avoid paying them. "I'm telling you he's trying to punk us by not paying. If you let him get away with it, next thing you know everybody will be trying that shit."

Charles leaned forward calmly. "Marion squared away his debt a few days ago," Charles said. He noticed the surprised look spread across his brother's face. "He apologized for the inconvenience and everything," he explained. "Now how he chooses to deal with people in his organization is none of my concern."

Jimmy was beside himself. He wasn't a stupid man. He knew Sonny's death only meant one thing, Marion was on to him. He didn't know how much Sonny had revealed before his death but Jimmy needed to eliminate Marion before his brother figured out what he had been up to. He had to kill him before Marion could make a move on him. But that was easier said than done. Marion moved smart, always surrounded by his henchmen.

Jimmy stared at Charles, then spoke, he tried to sound calm not wanting to tip his hand. "It's just something about him. I don't trust him."

Charles nodded but didn't say a word.

"He killed Sonny, his own guy. A nigga like that can't be trusted. He's a snake. I feel it in my gut. He only cares about money and he'll do anything to get it. If he'll do it to his own guys, he'll do it to us."

Charles remained silent. He seemed to be in deep thought as he watched his brother pace around the room.

Jimmy was immediately alarmed by his brother's silence. He was trying to read him but Charles gave him no clear indication of how he felt. Finally, Jimmy said, flatly, "I think we should kill him."

Charles eyed his brother suspiciously trying to understand where the sudden need to get rid of Marion was coming from. "What's all this really about?" He finally asked. "We are already spread thin being at war with the Martello family. That's where your focus should be," he told his brother. "Not this personal shit you got with Marion. What's your real beef with him anyway? You jealous?"

Charles words pissed him off but Jimmy played it cool. His brother's apprehension let him know exactly where he stood. "Jealous? Come on, Charles. You know me better than that. What the hell I got to be jealous about when it comes to that nigga. He only eating because we feeding him."

"Exactly," Charles said. "So what's wit all the hostility?"

"I just don't trust the nigga, that's all," Jimmy repeated. "You always taught me to only trust family. Blood over money, over power, over everything. That nigga ain't family."

"True indeed," Charles agreed. "But he's making us a whole lot of money. We got enough enemies to worry about. Can't start making one's out of our allies. So for now everything is cool. Just sit back and chill. I got this," he rose to his feet and put his hands on his little brother's shoulders. "I'm gonna keep a closer eye on him, now that you pulled my coat tail to it. I promise you. First sign of disloyalty I see, I'll kill him myself." Charles only meant what he said half-heartedly. Truth was, he wouldn't hesitate to kill Marion if he felt he couldn't trust him. But he did trust him, regardless of what Jimmy felt.

Emma stood at the top of the steps with a stunned look on her face, listening to their conversation. Filled with fear, her heart slowly fractured into to small pieces. She was distraught and still not able to comprehend what was happening. *"Why would Uncle Jimmy be trying to turn my father against Marion?"* she thought to herself. Marion had done nothing but showed loyalty to her father and her family. She cared so much about Marion, she thought about him constantly. It was much deeper than a crush or puppy love. He connected with her soul. No one could understand the bond she felt, not her father, not Ms. Tina and certainly not her Uncle Jimmy. She would do whatever she had to make sure no harm came his way.

Jimmy was her least favorite of all her uncles anyway. She began to curse him under her breath. Emma's heart and mind were broken. *How could her own family betray her like that*, she thought. All she saw was Marion in her future and now they wanted to murder him. There was a lump forming in her throat as she fought back tears. She felt helpless, just the thought of anything happening to him crushed her spirit. Emma was filled with bitterness and raced back to her room slamming the door as tears poured down her face. She laid across her bed and put her face in her pillow. She felt like she could just die. "I hate this house," she screamed into her pillow then continued crying hysterically. Marion had saved her life and now she felt the need to return the favor.

CHAPTER 9

Streaks of lightning brightened up the sky hiding the true color of the night accompanied by roars of thunder that shook the small studio apartment in Brooklyn. Marion laid still on the bed with his fingers locked behind his head. He was in deep thought, listening as the storm raged all around him. The powerful boom of thunder sounded like bombs going off, sending a jolt through his body and taking his mind back to his days spent in the jungles of Vietnam. Suddenly he could hear all the gunshots whizzing past his head and the tortured screams of the war. He saw the faces of fallen soldiers he had ate and laughed with, as well as the face of the men he had killed. The thick, pungent odor of death seemed to fill the room, choking him as it invaded his nostrils. The memories of his tour in Vietnam were all too vivid. The experience had changed him and had done the same to everyone he knew that had served. No one came out the same way they went in and a lot of the casualties of war were still amongst the living. The war had darkened the souls of men, instilling a kill or be killed mentality that was hard to turn off once they returned home. Marion was no different, he had just adapted his way of thinking to the drug game. He sat up in the bed, shaking the memories from his thoughts then focused his eyes on the rain streaking down the window. There was truly something about rainstorms that Marion loved. The thunder, the lightning, so much going on at once. In the midst of all that chaos, was when he did his best thinking, a trait that would serve him well as he rose through the ranks in the street.

A knock at the door broke Marion's concentration. Purely off instinct he grabbed his gun and crept to the door. Looking through the peephole, Marion couldn't believe his eyes. He tucked the gun in the small of his back and snatched open the door.

Emma stood in the doorway, soaked, tears escaping down her face mixing with the heavy rain. Her long, silky hair was now wet and wavy.

"What are you doing here?" Marion asked staring at her in astonishment.

"You have to go now," Emma blurted out.

"Huh?" A confused Marion responded.

"You have to get out of the city now. He wants to kill you," she spoke in a somber tone.

"He who?"

"My uncle," she explained. "I overheard him talking tonight," she wiped the tears that were running down her cheek. "He wants my father to let him kill you."

Marion grabbed her aggressively by the hand pulling her into the house and out of the rain. "Who knows you're here?" he asked sternly, sticking his head out the door and looking both ways before slamming it and locking it.

"Nobody," she sobbed. "I snuck out the house. I-I didn't know what else to do," she spoke in frantic spurts. "I couldn't stay there, I had to warn you. I don't ever want anything to happen to you. You have to run," Emma broke down collapsing into Marion's arms as he embraced her tightly.

"I ain't runnin' nowhere," he said confidently. "This has to be some type of misunderstanding." Marion was aware of Jimmy's hatred toward him but the fact that he had brought it to Charles attention caught him off guard. His mind began to churn with thoughts. "What did your father say?" Marion asked staring into Emma's eyes. *"Would she tell him the truth,"* he thought. He knew her loyalty lied with her father but the fact that she was at his door told Marion that she wanted him to trust her. And trust started with honesty.

"He didn't say much of anything. My uncle did most of the talking," Emma said. "Why is all this happening?" she asked, almost begging him for an answer. She was innocent, born into a life she didn't fully understand. She enjoyed all the spoils of being the daughter of such a powerful and well-respected man. But there was another side of the life that only until recently, she had begun to experience. Her father did a great job at keeping her sheltered over the years. But the war with the Martello family had exposed her to the grim and harsh reality of the underworld.

"Everything is gonna be ok," Marion told her. The wheels in his mind were still spinning.

"I feel like I can't breathe," she confessed. "I'm

suffocating in that house. My father is normally overprotective but he has tightened the screws since the incident that day."

"Can you blame him," Marion said truthfully only to receive an evil stare from Emma. "Your father is a man with great responsibilities but his greatest responsibility is you. If I were him, I would do everything in my power to make sure nothing ever happened to you."

"But this thing with my uncle—"

"Listen," Marion interrupted. "War brings out the best and worst in some people, trust me I know. I wish there was something more I could say to explain all of this. Something I could do to make it all go away. I would do anything to take away your pain and put a smile on your face," Marion said as he held her.

Emma looked up into his mesmerizing eyes as he spoke. His words resonated with her, she believed him. She loved the way she felt when in his presence, something about him gave her butterflies. She felt safe around him, the way she only had with her father.

Marion put his hand under her chin, "Why did you feel the need to tell me about your uncle? You know how this could look to your family. Why are you so willing to risk it all for me?" From the look in her eyes he already knew the answer but he wanted to hear her say it.

"Because," she said, her eyes falling to the ground again. She wanted to tell him because she thought about him every day. She wanted to say because he had captured her heart like no one had before. She wanted to scream out at the top of her lungs that she was in love with him and she meant it with all her heart. But he would think that she was just a silly girl overreacting to a crush, is what she told herself. So all she said was, "Because." For some reason Marion made her feel so unsure about herself when she was in his presence. Emma's nervous energy was always at an all-time high when he was around.

Marion could see right through her. Emma's eyes told what her mouth wouldn't say. "It's not safe for you to be roaming these streets by yourself," he told her. "Your family is at war. Your father would lose his mind if something was to happen to you. And he would be pissed if he knew you were here. I'm taking you home."

"So you're just like everybody else, afraid of my father," she snapped.

"I'm not afraid of anything," he said with such conviction Emma instantly believed him. "I'm just concerned for your safety."

"So you do care about what happens to me?" she asked.

Marion didn't hesitate or hide his feelings this time when he answered. "Yes. I care more than you know."

Emma's heart skipped a beat. "I feel safe here," Emma said rubbing her hand across his bare chest. His confidence was so sexy to her. He had quiet strength and a boss mentality about him that drew her in.

"You are," he said. "You are always safe with me."

To Marion, Emma was like the thunderstorms he loved so much, the one thing he could recall being both, beautiful and dangerous at the same time. Never one to shy away from danger, he grabbed her hand and kissed it.

Emma could feel the blood flowing through her body, swelling in places that had rarely been touched by anyone other than herself. In fact, she had grown tired of masturbating to thoughts of him, she wanted the real thing. She was yearning to be touched, Marion leaned forward and kissed her. Their lips locked naturally like they had done it numerous times. Emma let his tongue glide into her mouth.

They both enjoyed the sweetness of one another's tongues. The moment seemed to last forever. Marion's hands slid down to her waist as hers rose up his back. She wrapped her arms around him as he gripped her ass. She felt moisture in her panties, the warmth of his body pressing against her had her body on fire. Their tongues danced as Marion peeled her out of her wet clothing, one by one.

Emma soon found herself lying naked on the bed as Marion palmed her breast and kissed her neck. He caressed her body softly as he worked his hands south.

Emma was full of lust. "Marion," she called out as he slid his hands between her legs feeling her wetness.

Marion replaced his hand with his face, massaging her clit with his tongue causing Emma to let out a pleasurable sigh as she gripped the sheets. Her moans increased as he sucked on her flower bud until it was in full bloom. Emma felt her body tense up as she began to orgasm. The feeling was so intense. She had never experienced anything so pleasurable. He touched her like he knew her body better than her.

Marion's manhood was brick hard in his sweatpants as he stood up, staring down at her beautiful body. He stepped out of his sweats and Emma's eyes grew wide at the sight of his manhood. Marion was very well endowed. Even more than Emma had imagined. He climbed back on the bed between her legs, grabbing her thighs and pulling her to him. Marion rubbed his swollen mushroom head against her love spot before entering. He took his time, slowly easing into her not wanting to hurt her. She gasped as his girth filled her and her juices exploded from pure anticipation. He stroked her slowly as she wrapped her legs around him pulling him as far into her as she could. Emma wanted to feel every inch of him inside her. She wanted to lose herself in him. She wanted to pull him into her soul as he made love to her body. The passion they shared filled the room. Tears fell from Emma's eyes from pure ecstasy as she came again.

"Don't stop," she pleaded, feeling his love stick begin to throb inside her.

Marion didn't want to stop and he continued stroking until he spilled his seed inside of her. He collapsed on the bed next to her and she curled up onto his chest as he caressed the side of her face. It was something about Emma that Marion felt a strong connection to. It had only been made strong by the intimacy they had just shared. Marion knew he was in love and promised himself that he would love and care for her forever. He swore to protect her from harm, even if it cost him his life.

Emma was in love too and as she laid there in silence, she swore to herself that she would never leave Marion. She would love him for as long as they both lived, no matter what came their way. Until death did they part.

* * *

"I don't see why I can't just spend the night," Emma voiced her frustration as Marion pulled on her block. "You trying to get rid me?" she snapped.

"I got too much respect for you to do that," Marion charmed. "I also got respect for your father though. I just want to do this the right way. I refuse to disrespect what this could be. I wouldn't want some nigga keeping my daughter out all night, creeping around with her like some thief in the night. I'm not ashamed to claim you as mine to your father, your uncles or whoever," he said as he pulled over and parked in an empty spot just up the block from her brownstone. "And that's exactly what I plan to do, if that's alright with you," he asked then gave her a smile.

"Yes," she blushed. Emma was anxious to let their love

be known to everyone. If her family knew how much she loved him there would be no way her uncle would want Marion dead, even more importantly, there was no way her father would let it happen.

Marion exited the car then circled around to open her door. They walked up the block until they reach her brownstone. They walked up the steps but before they could reach the front door, it swung open and Charles Matthews stood in front of them dressed in silk pajamas. There was a menacing look of disapproval on his face as his glare shifted back and forth between Emma to Marion. He was flanked by an overzealous Jimmy, who looked a little too eager to do harm to Marion.

"What the fuck is going on here!" Charles didn't mince his words nor attempt to hide his anger. He was furious, "What are you doing with my daughter, Marion?"

"Daddy let me explain," Emma began only to be quickly cut off by her father's icy stare.

"What are you even doing out this house at this time of night, young lady," he barked at Emma, who lowered her head. "Now I'm gonna ask you again, why is she with you?" he said turning his attention back to Marion. "Are you fucking my daughter?" Charles asked through clenched teeth, the muscle in his jaw twitched as he stared at Marion.

"Of course he is," Jimmy joined in. "This nigga's a snake, I told you," he shouted.

If looks could kill, Jimmy would have dropped dead from the way Marion glanced at him.

"Don't lie to me," Charles warned Marion as Jimmy pulled the gun from his waist and cocked it. "Up until now, I've had the upmost respect for you. So don't lie to me."

"No daddy, I love him!" Emma shouted as tears flowed down her face.

"Take Emma in the house now," Charles commanded his brother.

"Marion!" she cried out as Jimmy attempted to grab her only to be stopped by Marion.

"Now," Charles said sternly looking at both Emma and Marion who were standing on his steps looking like Romeo and Juliet.

Marion pushed Jimmy's hand away then turned to a tearful Emma. "Do what your father says." When he saw her apprehension, he did his best to assure her that things would be alright. "It's okay, let us talk," he said then smiled at her and wiped the tears from her face.

Emma forced a smile then walked passed her father. Charles nostrils flared and his temper rose watching his daughter follow Marion's request rather than his.

"It doesn't matter what you do daddy, I won't stop loving him," Emma said as she walked pass her father into the house followed by Jimmy.

"I treated you like a son. How could you disrespect me like this?" Charles questioned as he eyed Marion intensely.

Marion remained cool. "That was never my intention," he replied. "I never expected any of this to happen but it did. I can't and I won't apologize for loving your daughter." Marion stood firm.

The young nigga had balls, Charles had to admit to himself. But right is right and wrong is wrong. And Marion was dead wrong. "You crossed the line. This thing between you and my daughter ends now. That's not a request and I won't tell you again." Charles said. "And our business together is over too," he informed Marion as Jimmy returned to the door with his gun in hand and two bodyguards. "I'm gonna let you live but I don't ever want to see your face again and my daughter don't either," Charles made his point clear.

Marion looked Jimmy in the face and they exchanged stares. Then he looked back at Charles and nodded his head before walking down the steps and up the block.

"I told you about that nigga. I was right the whole time." Jimmy bragged in a celebratory manner. Only to feel his brother's still simmering wrath.

"Shut the fuck up, Jimmy." Charles demanded.

Jimmy quickly straightened up. His face got serious and he asked, "You…You want me to take care of him?"

Charles stared up the block at Marion. There was a long pause before he spoke, "Nah, leave him be, for now.

Kingdom Come

CHAPTER 10

The rain had slowed and the street lights were shining off the wet pavement as Marion pulled onto his block and parked. He stepped out of the car, onto the street and walked around to the sidewalk. Almost simultaneously, an Italian man in a suit approached him from the front and two hulking goons boxed him in from behind, placing their guns in his back. Marion lifted his hands.

"My boss would like to speak with you," the man in the suit said as he reached into Marion's jacket and relieved him of his weapon.

"Is that right," Marion answered arrogantly still pissed from what had happened back at Emma's house. Before he could say another word he felt a bag slip over his head. "What the…" the sound of his voice muffled. Marion began to put up a fight trying to struggle his way free but the two goons easily overpowered him. Still he kept fighting until a punch to the gut caused him to doubled over, knocking the wind out of him. "Arrhh," he grunted from the blow.

"Got damn, he's strong as an ox," Marion heard one of the men say. He felt a thump on the side of his head sending him crumpling to the ground, suddenly as if someone had pulled a set of curtains over his eyes, his world went dark.

※ ※ ※

Marion groaned as he slowly regained consciousness he could feel the burn from the tightly tied rope digging into his wrist. He was confined to a chair with his arms bound behind his back. The bag was no longer over his head but the room was pitch black, making it impossible to see his surroundings. There was an uncomfortable chill in the room and he could hear music playing in the distance, along with voices but they were inaudible. He felt groggy, disorientated and it took him a few minutes to get his bearings. A loud humming sound filled the room. *Maybe from an air conditioner or cooler,* Marion thought to himself, still a bit confused as to what was going on. He jerked forward causing the chair to screech loudly across the concrete floor as he tried to free himself. The more he moved his hands against the ropes, the more they cut into the skin around his wrist. Once again he lurched forward forcefully, the series of movements causing the chair to sway and wobble before it tilted over. Marion crashed into a bunch of boxes knocking everything over landing on his side. *Shit, they heard me,* he thought to himself hearing a heavy footfall on the stairs and seeing a glimmer of light come into the room from under the door. When the footsteps reached the bottom of the stairs the heavy steel door pushed open and two men burst into the dimly lit room. One of the men strutted over to where Marion laid and stood directly over him. He pulled the beaded metal chain turning on a lightbulb that hung just above him. The bright light swung back and forth causing Marion to squint his eyes before he was finally able to focus. Looking around, he saw rows of oak wine barrels lining the walls and realized he was in a wine cellar beneath a restaurant.

"Pick him up," a voice ordered from the top of the stairs and the men did as they were told.

Marion heard another set of footsteps coming down the steps and a well-dressed, middle-aged man entered his view. Using a cloth napkin to wipe his mouth and hands, he walked over to Marion and knelt beside him. "Nice seeing you again kid," the man said, his warm breath smelled like wine and garlic.

Marion studied the man in front of him. His hair was sprinkled with more specs of grey than he remembered but was still thick and full. He was a bit thinner but still had a beak like nose and a hard face, only now there were wrinkles lines around his eyes.

"Mr. Brigandi," Marion's tone was one of surprise but not worry.

"Mr. Brigandi, Mr. Brigandi," the Don repeated in his hoarse voice and thick Italian accent. "What's with all the formal stuff? I thought I was Uncle Carlo?" he said in a jovial tone.

"That was a long long time ago," Marion said remaining stoned face as he stared at the legendary mobster who sat on the Mount Rushmore of organized crime. Carlo Brigandi controlled and dominated the heroin trades in Brooklyn and Queens. Marion hadn't seen him in years and couldn't understand what the sudden reunion was about.

Carlo Brigandi patted Marion on his knee then stood up straight. "You know me and your father, God bless his soul," he paused making the sign of the cross over his chest and head before continuing, "There's only been a few men on this earth that I respected like I did your father. He was a man's man. He spent over a decade in the big house for something I did and he never rolled, ratted or complained, not once."

"I know the story," Marion responded. "He also died broke in jail. You always leave that part out."

A thin smirk creased Carlo's lips. "Where I come from loyalty is everything and the loyalty your father showed me makes us family."

"If this is how you treat family then," Marion retorted letting his words trail off, looking down at his restraints and feeling the throbbing knot on the back off his head.

"My apologies. These guys have to learn to be more diplomatic in their duties," Carlo said looking back at his goons. "Untie him," he instructed them and continued talking. "Why haven't you been to see me since you've gotten out the army?"

Marion smirked and shrugged his shoulders, clearly the old man had been keeping tabs on him. "What's so urgent that we needed to meet like this?" Marion asked, rubbing his freshly freed wrist.

"Walk with me," Carlo told him.

The two of them walked through a door that led out to an empty lot behind the restaurant. Marion looked back over his shoulders at Brigandi's two goons that followed close behind but out of earshot.

"This war between Charles Matthews and the Martello family has gone on far too long. Every other day it seems like one of their soldiers are being gunned down it the street. All this negative press is not good for business, for the Italians or the Blacks," Carlo explained walking with his hands behind his back. "Me, along with some other members of The Commission feel that if this war is allowed to continue, it won't be long before we're all out of business. Martello is an old stubborn fuck. He won't stop until Charles is dead. Only problem is, he is the leader of an incompetent bunch of fuck ups who keep missing their target. From a distance, because I don't know him, Charles seems like a man that is stuck in his ways as well. So this seems like a never ending situation."

Marion nodded to show his understanding.

"Somebody has to end it for them," Carlo said truthfully. "So I have an opportunity for you. A chance of a lifetime."

Marion kept a poker face as Carlo did his best to sell him on whatever it was he was about to offer.

"I'm offering you the chance to move up in the world. Be the next Charles Matthews, even bigger." Carlo explained then added almost nonchalantly. "All you have to do is…"

"Kill Charles Matthews right," Marion replied finishing Carlo's sentence already anticipating where the old man was going.

Marion immediately saw Emma's face pop into his mind. He couldn't possibly hurt her like that. Besides, Charles had put him on, giving him an opportunity to eat like no other hustler in the city. He had treated him like a son, guiding him on his rise. Marion had a solid plan when he left the army but it was his chance encounter with Charles Matthews that made it all come together. Marion felt like a snake even having this discussion.

"Let me ask you something," Marion said as they continued to walk. "What made you decided that Charles had to be the one that dies. Why not Martello? You said there are other members of The Commission that are against his personal war. Why not do yourselves a favor and kill him," Marion wanted to know.

"The lesser of two evils," Carlo said truthfully. "I kill Martello; it'll start a war between The Five Families. Besides, if Martello wins, the other families and myself would get a piece of the action."

"So it's a business decision," Marion retorted.

"It's always a business decision." Carlo replied.

"Look, Charles Matthews gave me my opportunity," Marion said as he stopped walking and faced Don Brigandi. "You spoke about my father and his loyalty to you. You still respect him to this day. But here you are asking me to betray Charles Matthews."

"I understand that, but now put yourself in Charlie's shoes. If he was standing right here and I gave him the exact same offer, what would he do?" Carlo asked. "You think he would spare you?"

Marion knew it was a dirty game. Would Charles kill him for a chance at being the man? "*Probably. Shit, definitely,*" he thought to himself. He had killed men for less, but Charles had just spared Marion's life over Emma. On top of that, Marion's principle beliefs wouldn't let him do it. He wasn't going to bend those rules for money or power.

Marion studied Carlo for a minute before giving his answer. "I'm gonna have to respectfully pass."

Carlo stared at him. "What is it kid? I know you want to do it. I know you want to be a top guy in this business. It's written all over you. Anybody with eyes can see it," Carlo expressed. "What's holding you back?"

What was holding Marion back was his love for Emma. She had become his weakness like she was her father's. She seemed to have that effect on all the men in her life.

"It's the girl isn't it?" Carlo sneered. It was like he read it in Marion's eyes. Marion was in love. "Got dammit kid," Carlo said full of disappointment. "I've seen that look before. I had that same dumb look in my eyes when I met my wife. Listen to me," he stressed his point by increasing his voice but quickly raised his hand to his men instructing them to remain calm. "This is a chance of a lifetime you're leaving on the table here. Don't do it."

"My answer is my answer," Marion said coolly.

Carlo shook his head. He knew Marion was just a kid,

still a baby barely in his twenties, who thought he had it all figured out. "What's with all this love shit? You came back from Vietnam a hippie?" Carlo quipped. "Don't be stupid kid. I'm giving you a chance to get on the right side of this thing. Think with your head not your heart and certainly not your dick."

Marion stared at Carlo in silence.

"She's a beautiful girl," Carlo admitted. "But there are plenty of beautiful girls in the world. Especially when you're one of the top guys."

"Am I free to go?" Marion asked becoming annoyed with the discussion.

"Listen Marion and listen up good," Carlo said as his voice grew calm. "One of the hardest things in life is knowing which bridges to cross and which ones to burn. Kill Charles Matthews and you'll have everything you ever wanted. You'll become the most powerful black gangster in the city."

Marion looked away, giving the impression he was giving second thought to the offer but he never wavered between choices. Things had changed for him and he was unwavering in his loyalty, which he had pledged to Emma, along with his love that ran much deeper than Carlo could imagine. "I know what I'm doing."

Carlo Brigandi slowly nodded his head. He knew deep down inside Marion would never agree to his deal. He was stubborn, it was in his DNA to stand firm on what he believed. Carlo couldn't help but to respect that. "Ok kid, at least I tried," he said as he hugged Marion and kiss both of his cheeks. He stepped aside allowing Marion to pass, signaling to his men that it was okay to let him leave, unharmed. When Marion made it a few feet away, Carlo called out to him, "Hey kid, make sure I get an invitation to the wedding," he joked.

Marion looked back and smiled but never said a word, he disappeared around the building.

"You gotta give it to him boss," one of Carlo's goons said. "The kid's got balls the size of a bull and he's loyal as a seeing eyes dog," he laughed.

"To a fault," Carlo replied. "But he's young, he'll learn."

CHAPTER 11

It was late and Josie stood behind the bar at Nelle's, wiping down the countertop. It had been another long night and she couldn't have been happier that it was nearing closing time. Hours earlier the bar was packed with patrons shouting and cheering as they watched Game 7 of the NBA Finals between the Seattle Supersonics and the Washington Bullets. It had been a good night financially for Josie, who had purchased the bar a few years ago from the original owner. The drinks were flowing as the customers watched the game with rousing interest but now it was empty and quiet. She finally dried the last beer mug then wiped her hands with a dry towel. When she looked up, a man was entering the bar. Josie looked up at the clock and sighed, it was four minutes before closing. She whispered underneath her breath, "You can't be serious," then walked from around the counter to intercept the man before he could reach the bar. "I'm sorry sir but we're closed," she said.

"I just came to collect on a bet," he replied.

Josie hesitated briefly. The man looked disheveled and down on his luck. His breath smelled like liquor and his clothes were over worn. She thought he was a drunk that had stumbled in.

"I won big on the game tonight," the man said joyfully. "Real, real big and I came to collect."

Josie shook her head. Her husband Goose was the neighborhood bookie and all types of people came to the bar to place bets with him. He ran his business from the bar's back office.

"Wait right here," she told the man. Then turned and headed to the office to get Goose.

"Goose," she called out.

The bar's office barely had any furniture in it, just the

desk where Goose sat and a few file cabinets up against the wall. Goose was in the process of counting money and didn't bother to look up at his wife when she entered calling his name. "What's up?" he replied.

"There's some guy out there saying he came to collect on a bet," Josie said.

"What's his name?" Goose asked finally looking up.

"Didn't ask," Josie said. That was his business and she really didn't get involved. "Could you please come handle it because I'm ready to go home," she pleaded then gave him the puppy eyes and pouted her lip.

He smiled and stood up from his desk. "I got it babe," he said like he was her hero then smacked her on the ass as he walked pass.

"That's gonna get you in trouble," she teased as she followed him out the office.

"I hope so," he flirted back as they walked down the hallway.

When Goose reached the bar area, he felt his knees almost give out when he saw what was waiting on him. Standing near the bar, along with five of his men, was Jimmy Matthews sporting a menacing smirk on his face. He, along with all his men, were armed with handguns.

"Oh my God," Josie screamed and froze with fear.

"Hey, what's all this shit about Jimmy," Goose said as he put his arm around Josie and pushed her behind him, shielding her.

"Marion," Jimmy spewed with venom in his tone. "He fucked up. Couldn't keep his dick in his pants."

"All this is over some broad?" Goose replied still a bit confused. "C'mon Jimmy, you know how the game go. You not being a playa about this shit, at all."

"This ain't over no broad," Jimmy barked angrily. "This is about my niece, Emma. All the women in this city and he just couldn't stay away from just one. Rule number one, the boss' daughter is always off limits."

Goose had a look of surprise on his face. He had no idea about the relationship between Marion and Emma. Jimmy picked up on that.

"Oh, you didn't know," he chuckled. "Yo' boss out here putting yo' life in danger and you didn't even know," Jimmy shook his head. "Where is he?" Jimmy asked cutting straight to it.

"I have no idea," Goose said.

"Even if you did you wouldn't tell me anyway," Jimmy said.

"Nah, I wouldn't. Marion been on to your shit. We know you was behind the robbery," Goose said. His chest swelled with anger as he looked into Josie's fright filled face. "Wait until your brother finds out you been stealing from him. He definitely gonna hear about this," Goose said.

Jimmy laughed. "How you know he don't already know? How you know he's not the one that sent me," Jimmy lied convincingly. "Too bad you'll never get those answers."

As the words left his lips all his men lifted their guns and began to fire at Goose and Josie, swiss cheesing the both of them. Josie let out a high pitched ear piercing cry as the shots ripped through her. The hail of bullets pushed Goose back up against the wall, the shots seemed to keep both of them up right until the firing stopped. Goose's bloody, bullet riddled body fell lifelessly to the ground followed by Josie's slumped on top of him. By the time the shooting had ceased the bar looked like a shooting range.

* * *

Marion had a lot on his mind and drove straight to Nelle's after his impromptu meeting with Carlo Brigandi. He immediately paused when he reached the door of the bar. Seeing it left wide open gave him an eerie feeling and he instantly knew something was wrong. He pulled out his gun and slowly entered the bar. Moving cautiously through the dimly lit hallway with his head on a swivel, Marion approached the bar area. His heart suddenly dropped into his stomach when he saw the blood spattered carnage and the bullet-ridden bodies of Goose and Josie. He closed his eyes for a second to regulate his breathing. He had seen his fair share of corpses, but this was much different. These belonged to one of his oldest friends and the cousin who he loved like a sister. There was hatred in his eyes and his face was streaked with tears as he looked into Josie's lifeless eyes. "I'm sorry," he leaned over and closed Josie's eyelids, unable to withstand the guilt he felt from her dead eyes staring at him. All at once, a deadly vengeance swept over Marion. He wasn't exactly sure who was behind Goose and Josie's death but he had a few ideas. *"Was this Charles Matthews' message for disrespecting his family? Or was it the result of turning down Carlo Brigandi's offer? Or was it some other mobsters who wanted to teach him a lesson."* he thought to himself. Either way Marion knew he was somehow responsible for the deaths of Goose and Josie. Now he knew he could no longer afford to remain neutral in the war. Not anymore.

* * *

Two days later Marion summoned Nate to meet him at his apartment. The two had convened plenty of times but Nate could feel the difference in this meeting as soon as he walked in. Marion was normally difficult to read but not on this day. His pain and anger was obvious.

"What the hell's going on?" Nate asked, his eyebrows wrinkled and lines forming on his forehead. He felt the tension in the room and could see the stress on Marion's face.

"Have a seat Skate," Marion said.

Nate took a seat in a wooden chair across from where Marion sat down. "What's up mane," he said in his country drawl. "You look like you got some real heavy shit weighin' on you."

"Somebody killed Josie and Goose the other night." Marion came right out with it.

"Got damn me," Nate shouted as he snatched his hat off and slammed it to the ground. "Goose and Josie? What was it a robbery or some shit?"

"Nah, wasn't no robbery," Marion was sure of his statement. "It was definitely a hit."

Nate rubbed the top of his head. "Who you think did it?"

Marion shook his head slowly and shrugged his shoulders. "I been going back and forth on it all night. Could be the Italians. Could be Charles. I'm not sure," he said shaking his head in frustration.

"Charles?" Nate sounded stunned. "Jimmy, yeah I can see but why the fuck would Charles have a beef with you?"

"His daughter," Marion revealed.

"Shit, nigga," Nate's voiced boomed. "You fucked her didn't you?" he shook his head. "I knew you was. I hope the pussy was worth it. I told you that girl was bad news. The worst kind of bad news, knowmtalmbout?"

Marion didn't respond. He didn't care for Nate's opinion on the situation with Emma at the moment, he switched the subject. "That ain't what I called you here to talk about," he said.

"Shit, it's more?" Nate asked assuming that was the worst of it.

"This war between Charles and Martello has to end,"

Marion declared. "I'm not sure who killed Goose and Josie but what I do know is we ain't prepared to go to war with either one of them right now, if they were responsible," he truthfully admitted. "But Martello won't stop until Charles is six feet deep in the ground," Marion told Nate.

"And Charles won't stop either," Nate said.

"Exactly," Marion agreed. "That's why we're gonna end the war for him."

Nate leaned forward in his chair extremely interested. "I'm all ears," he said.

"If I can get rid of Martello, Charles will forever be indebted to me," Marion said but what he didn't say was that he was attempting the underlay for the overplay, hoping that by killing Don Martello, he would earn Charles' blessing when it came to his daughter. "With Martello out the way," Marion continued, "Charles gets to keep control of his territory and takes over the parts of Harlem that Martello controls. We get our connect back and we back in business, better than ever."

Nate leaned back in his chair, grinning from ear to ear. "I gotta give it to you. That's a helluva plan. Getting rid of Martello won't be easy though," Nate admitted. "But if you pull this shit off, you're one cold ass muthafucka." Nate laughed, then suddenly eyed Marion suspiciously before saying, "I know you, nigga. You're a thinking man. I know there's a bigger play at work here. I just haven't figured it out yet."

Marion's face creased with a smile that gradually grew wider. "You know what Skate, we the only ones playing by the rules," Marion explained. "But what I realized is ain't no rules in this shit. If you got enough money, enough power or enough guts, any rule can be broken." Marion knew his plan was foolproof, actually it was pure genius. He was playing chess and he was just lining his piece up for his best move yet.

Kingdom Come

CHAPTER 12

Shopping was the thing that Joseph Martello loved to do the most. He got an erotic charge from it that only the adrenaline rush of war could match. It was something about the hunt, finding the perfect suit was like tracking down someone that had to be killed and to complete the mission was like pure ecstasy. The Don was definitely a dapper, well-kept gangster, with an outspoken personality. He wore nothing but the best; expensive fabrics and tailored suits. He loved to be the center of attention, while most bosses shunned the spotlight, Don Martello lusted after it. He was the same way when it came to shopping, he loved to see salespeople falling all over themselves to serve his every need. The Don was excessive in almost everything he did, from his flamboyant lifestyle to his hunger for control of the drug trade in Harlem. His appetite didn't stop with his pursuit of power, evident by his rotund waistline. He had been waging war with Charles Matthews for almost a year now and he had no plans of stopping. Not even all of the heat he was attracting could deter him. He got a kick out of all the headlines. He routinely made his underlings read his press clippings to him.

"I love this," the Don's voice boomed as he looked at himself in the multiple full length mirrors that surrounded him. He stretched his arms out and spun around. "Whadda you think Silvio?" he asked his underboss who nodded his approval. "I'll take this one and the other two as well," he informed his tailor as he lifted his arms so the man could help him remove the suit jacket.

"I'll make the proper adjustments and have them sent over to you immediately sir," the tailor said obediently nodding as he removed the jacket and moving aside allowing Martello to pass.

The Don waddled across the thick silk carpeting of the

private dressing area to a private fitting room. He sat down on the soft-silk covered wood bench and began taking off the pair of slack that he had tried on.

BANG! BANG!

The sound of gunfire was followed by terrified screams and pleas from the people outside the private fitting room. Suddenly, the door to Don Martello's fitting room swung open violently and he found himself staring into a double barrel shotgun.

"Do you know who I am?" Martello shouted furiously looking up at Marion. "You're a fucking dead man," he barked. Then he peeked around Marion and could see Nate standing over the bodies of Silvio, his underboss and the rest of his bodyguards, lying on the floor in a pool of blood. Don Martello stared into Marion's eyes, he could see the grim reaper staring back. At that moment, he knew he would not live to see another day but still he tried negotiating for his life. "Who sent you?" Martello inquired. "How much are they paying you? I'll triple it," he promised in a pleading tone.

"Somethings are worth more to a man than money," Marion said.

"You're a fool," Martello laughed. "Nothing is worth

more than money." When Marion didn't respond the Don continued, "Do you have any idea what my people are going to do to you, you fuckin' moulinyan. I'm not the kind of man you can do something like this to and expect to get away with it," the Don sneered.

"Let's see." Marion smirked. The shotgun in his hand roared thunderously, cutting Joseph Martello nearly in half. The blast lifted the Don's large frame up out of his seat and sent him crashing through the dressing room wall.

Marion stepped through the door, standing over Martello's body. There was a hole the size of a large dinner plate in his chest and blood leaking from the side of his mouth. Marion reached down snatched the silk designer scarf from around the dead man's neck before turning and exiting.

* * *

Marion went straight to see Charles Matthews as soon as the Martello hit was done. He paused when he reached the steps of the Matthews home. On the outside he looked calm but on the inside he felt a bit unsettled. He felt like he was approaching an active volcano as he walked towards the door and he wasn't sure if it was about to erupt or not. Marion banged on the door, when it opened he was greeted by two guns being shoved in his face. The eagerness to kill was plastered on the faces of the men holding the weapons and Marion braced for the shot he knew could come at any moment.

"I need to see Charles!" he said emphatically.

"Look at this shit here," Marion recognized Jimmy's voice coming from behind the two guards before he even saw him. "I thought you were told never to show your face around here again."

"I need to see Charles, right now," Marion repeated.

Jimmy could see traces of blood spattered on his clothes and was briefly taken aback. "What the fuck do you want!' he shouted.

"I got some information I'd think he'd like to know," Marion said.

"Bring that nigga in here," Jimmy commanded the two gun toting bodyguards who snatched Marion in the door.

Emma heard the commotion at the front door from her room, she raced out into the hallway and screamed when she reached the top of the stairs seeing Marion being led into the house at gunpoint by her uncle and a pair of bodyguards.

"Marion!" She cried out as Ms. Tina came to her aid, grabbing her around the waist and restraining her from going down the steps. Emma's heart ached. "No!" She shouted as tears filled her eyes and began to fall. She broke away from Ms. Tina and bolted down the stairs but was stopped by one of the guards before she could get to Marion.

Jimmy turned on his heels. "Take your ass back upstairs," he yelled at Emma with so much arrogance and bravado that it took everything in Marion to keep from reacting.

"Get your hands off my daughter," Charles voice roared through the air as time seemed to freeze.

Emma snatched away from the bodyguard as he loosened his grip on her then ran over to her father.

"I'm sorry Mr. Matthews," the guard humbly apologized.

Emma embraced her father burying her head in his chest. "Daddy please don't hurt him," she begged, tears covering her face as she looked up at him with saddened eyes. Her heart was pounding, feeling as it would leap from her chest and Charles could feel it as she squeezed him tighter.

Marion hadn't seen Emma since he had brought her home that night and the sight of her made his heart race. Even in her distressed circumstance, her beauty still shined through.

Charles' piercing glare landed on Marion, who returned a stare just as intense. Each man refusing to blink or look away. It was a battle of wills and the tension threatened to choke the air out of the room.

Charles peeled his daughter's arms from around him. His cold stare told Emma all she needed to know, Marion was in dire straits and his life hung in the balance. "Tina," Charles called out. "Take Emma back up to her room." He waved his two fingers directing the men holding Marion to follow him.

"No! Daddy! No!" Emma sobbed and screamed for her father as he turned to walk in his office. Jimmy was last to enter and smirked at Emma as he closed the door behind the group of men.

"C'mon baby," Ms. Tina said trying to console her but she pushed her away. Ms. Tina managed to wrap Emma in her embrace as a flood of emotions swept over the young women. She could feel all of Emma's weight collapse on her as she rubbed her back.

"They can't kill him," Emma pleaded for Ms. Tina to do something as she led her away.

Charles entered the room leaned his back up against his

desk and folded his arms. "I thought I made myself crystal clear the last time we saw each other," he said sternly. "I'm not a man who likes repeating himself."

Marion looked around the room at every Matthews brother and a few more bodyguards. He knew that he was in the middle of the lion's den and he had to choose his words carefully. "I understand that but I got some information I'm sure you'll be interested in hearing," Marion said.

"I better be, you risked your life coming here," Charles said. His face remained emotionless and his eyes trained on Marion. He motioned for Jimmy to hand him his gun, he chambered a round. "You got 60 seconds to tell me why you're here or I'm gonna put a bullet in your head myself."

"I wanna show you something," Marion said. Then he slowly and cautiously reached into his jacket. The sound of guns being pulled filled the room like a small audience clapping. Marion froze seeing every gun in the room aimed at him. He looked at Charles who nodded, allowing him to reach into his jacket. Marion pulled the bloody scarf from inside the jacket and held it out in front of him.

"What the hell is that?" Charles asked not understanding the meaning of the bloody cloth.

"This is Joseph Martello and the Martello family waving their white flag," Marion smirked as he shook the scarf.

Charles raised his eyebrow still a bit confused. "What the fuck is this, some kind of joke?"

"I don't have much of a sense of humor," Marion replied. "Turn on the TV."

Charles nodded to one of his men, who walked over and clicked on the television set. The news of Don Joseph Martello's murder in a men's boutique in Manhattan was on almost every channel. Charles walked around his desk and took a seat. He instantly felt like a burden had been lifted off of him and every man in the room felt the same. The 10-month war had taken a toll on all of them mentally, physically and financially. Charles placed his hand on his chin and stared at Marion but now his gaze was one of amazement. The young man in front of him had singlehandedly pulled off what he hadn't been able to do, kill his biggest rival.

Marion could feel the tension in the room slowly began to subside. Their frigid glares melted the same way Charles' had, all but Jimmy's, of course.

"I guess I owe you huh, kid? Big time," Charles smiled. "Name a price. What you want money, bricks, just name it and it's yours."

"Take advantage kid, he's not usually this charitable," one of the Matthews brothers joked.

"What'll it be?" Charles said pouring a couple glasses of cognac. He walked back around the desk and handed one to Marion.

Marion accepted and took a sip. Then he looked Charles directly in his eyes and said, "All I want is your blessing." He pulled a ring box from his pocket and flipped it open.

Charles looked at the flawless diamond inside the box, then back up at Marion and a smiled spread across his face.

Kingdom Come

CHAPTER 13

3 Months Later

"Let's make a plan," Marion said smoothly as Emma stood motionless with her hands covering her tear filled face. "Twenty years from today, we'll tell our children the story of how their parents fell in love and got married," he said finishing his toast then sipping his champagne. There wasn't a dry eye in the entire room.

The reception took place in a grand ballroom inside the Waldorf Astoria hotel in Manhattan. Charles Matthews had to pull some strings to gain access to the elegant ballroom. Marion, Emma and the rest of the wedding party sat at a long table on a raised stage in the front of the room. The rest of the dining hall was occupied by beautifully decorated round tables. Emma's uncles sat closest to the stage and followed Marion's speech with their own, proposing a toast to the bride and groom, wishing them years of happiness, wealth and many children amongst other things. By now, Emma was bawling and unable to speak, her hands were trembling from the outpouring of love. Marion put his glass down on the table and pulled her into his embrace.

"I love you, Emma Holloway," he said then kissed her as their guest all cheered then sipped their champagne.

"That has a nice ring to it," she replied smiling through her tears of joy.

Charles Matthews had spent lavishly on the wedding of his princess. The father of the bride stood off to the side beaming with pride. Charles had never seen his daughter look more beautiful and he was taking in everything about the joyous celebration. His only wish was that his wife could have been there to see her.

From his chair on the raised stage, Marion watched all of

the wedding guest. At one table sat Felix Santos, stuffing his face with a large napkin tucked in the front of his suit. Seated at the table with him were his son, Andres and a few of their henchmen. They had all attended as a show of respect to the father of the bride. Everyone seemed to be enjoying the festive atmosphere, all except Jimmy Matthews. He was seated at the table with the rest of Emma's uncles, glaring spitefully at Marion. Leaning back in his seat Jimmy's chest was puffed out and his facial expression was filled with scorn.

Charles watched their interaction from afar and shook his head. He was planning on having a family sit-down soon after the wedding to straighten things out between the two of them. He wanted to avoid any friction within the family moving forward. When Charles caught Marion's eyes he waved his hand calling him over.

"I'll be right back," Marion whispered to Emma.

"Is everything alright?" She asked, gently touching Marion's hand.

Marion leaned in and kissed her, then smiled. "Everything is perfect," he said then got up.

"Come with me," Charles told Marion before turning and walking away. "You're part of this family now and I want you to be able to provide the type of lifestyle for yourself and my daughter that she is accustom to," Charles explained as they walked.

Marion followed until he found himself inside one of the offices at the reception hall. The room was void of any furniture, except for a few folded chairs leaning against the wall. To his surprise Felix and Andres Santos stood in the middle of the room. They greeted both men as they entered with a nod of the head.

Charles closed the door behind them then turned to Marion, who gave him a suspicious look. "I want to give you a personal wedding gift. Something just for you," Charles said. "You no longer have to go through me. From now on, you will be dealing directly with Felix and his son." He was introducing Marion directly to the connect, something he hadn't even done for his brothers. "You are my son now and family looks out for family. I'm gonna help you take over Brooklyn, the way I did Harlem," Charles beamed as he spoke to his new son in law.

"I'm starting you off with 25 kilos on consignment to be delivered to wherever ju want. All ju have to do is name the place and we go into business," Felix informed Marion.

"That's it?" Marion asked cool, calm and unfazed.

"That's it," Charles replied. "They'll be waiting for you when you get back from your honeymoon."

"What's the catch?" Marion quizzed.

"No catch, no strings. It's a gift," Charles explained. "A birthright, like welcome to the family."

Marion paused for a moment. The thought of getting his hands on 25 bricks, brought the hustler in him to a boil. Charles was offering him something he always wanted, independence. This was a real opportunity of a lifetime. No percentage, no nothing, just his daughter's security. Marion's father had remained loyal to Carlo Brigandi and what had it gotten for him, nothing. He died broke and in jail for a crime he didn't committed. That was the harsh truth, no matter how the Don tried to spin it into a tale of honor. Marion believed his father was honorable as well. He also believed the streets owed his old man a debt and he was going to collect on that debt with interest in a way that had been denied to his father. Those 25 kilos were the first step. He knew he could take over his city.

"927 Prospect Place in Brooklyn," Marion said to Felix, "You need me to write it down?"

"No, I got it," Andres interjected. "Your family and mine have made lots of money together. My father and I look forward to that continuing in the future," he said then shook Marion's hand firmly. "Give Emma my love," he said.

"Yes, please," Felix said. "And express to her how sorry I am that we couldn't stay," he said before shaking both men's hands and exiting along with his son.

The room fell silent momentarily, both men just staring at the door the Santos' had exited. Finally, Charles spoke. "You know it's something else I been meaning to talk to you about. This thing between you and Jimmy," but he paused as the other Matthews Brothers, except the aforementioned Jimmy, suddenly entered the room.

All the men were dressed to the nines and stared approvingly at Marion with proud smiles on their faces but none were bigger than his new father in law.

"We just wanted to formally welcome you into the family," one of the brothers said joyfully as he put his hands on Marion's shoulders. "Once you're in there's no getting out," he said causing them all to laugh.

"From this day forward, if you have a problem of any kind, you can bring it to me," Charles declared, speaking like a true Godfather.

Marion nodded his reply.

Charles extended his hand out to Marion. "I always wanted a son," he bragged with a prideful smile etched on his face. Marion returned the smile and shook his hand as Charles pulled him in for a hug. "Now let's celebrate," Charles shouted as the group of men exited the room returning to the festivities.

"What was that all that about?" Emma asked with a concerned look on her face as Marion returned to the table. "Is everything alright?" she questioned again before he had a chance to answer her first question.

"Yeah," Marion answered. "Andres Santos sends his love," he said with a sly grin.

Emma gave him a coy smile and leaned in. "Let's dance my love," she said sweetly.

* * *

It was almost midnight when the party broke. Many of the family members and guest had cleared out, leaving behind a mess for the catering service to clean up. A slightly drunk Charles sat at a table surrounded by his brothers and new son-in-law, the caterers scrambled around them disassembling tables and chairs, trying to return the reception hall back to its original appearance. The crew in charge of the floral arrangements were racing back and forth as well, removing the huge baskets of exotic flowers, placing them in a large truck parked out front. A half empty bottle of liquor rested in the middle of the table as the men took shots, laughed loudly and relaxed.

"Look at you. You fit right in," Emma said as she approached the table and tapped her new husband on the shoulder. "I'm getting a little tired," she expressed, code for she was ready to leave.

The group rose to their feet, exchanging hugs and handshakes with the newlyweds. Charles was last to stand up. He hugged and kissed Emma over and over, still amazed at how beautiful she looked in her wedding dress.

"I can't believe my baby's a married woman," he said. "Your mother would have been proud to see you and the woman you have grown into. I'm proud of you."

"I know daddy," Emma replied as tears welled up in her eyes. She had tried avoiding the subject of her mother all day.

An exuberant smile appeared on Charles face as he turned

to Marion, "Congratulations, my son and once again, welcome to the family."

All the Matthew brothers, even Jimmy converged on Marion embracing him, accepting him as one of their own.

"Ok, I know ya'll are drunk now," Emma teased at their group hug.

"Ok we gotta go," Marion said looking at his watch and realizing how late it had gotten. "We leave for the Dominican Republic bright and early in the morning."

"Enjoy your honeymoon," Charles said as the two of them headed for the car. "Damn I can't believe my baby girl is really married," Charles repeated to himself shaking his head before taking a seat and pouring the group another round of shots. His chest swelled with a sense of achievement and gratification knowing he had done his best raising his daughter. He knew she would be a good wife to Marion. Emma understood the line of work her husband was in. She had been around it her whole life. Charles had cut into Marion from the first day he had come to his house. What he saw in the kid lead him to believe that Marion had boss potential, he just needed some grooming. Instead of smothering it and snuffing it out, Charles had decided to facilitate it. With the war against the Martello family in his rearview, he could now focus on rebuilding strength all around him. As Marion would grow, the more powerful Charles' organization would become, if and when it went up against The Commission. Something he was sure would happen in the future. It was all strategic. He lifted his glass and gulped down the cognac. He poured another and raised his glass once again, "This one is for Pee Wee," he told them. His brothers held their glasses up to toast him then turned up their drinks.

Charles heart immediately sank into his stomach when he looked up and saw two of the flower crew approaching the table with masks over their faces. The men had automatic weapons in their hands. At the same moment, four more masked caterers barged into the reception hall armed with handguns. Time seemed to grind to a halt, Charles felt it in his heart, this was the end. His only feeling was one of remorse not fear. Not remorse for anything he had done in his lifetime, the remorse he felt was for Emma. He knew his death would leave a hole in her life and a scar on her heart that would never heal, even with Marion there to take care of her. It was as though his entire life flashed before his eyes. He saw Emma being born all over again, he saw her first steps and heard her speak her first words. He saw images of him teaching her how to ride a bike and saw her enjoying her first dance with her husband. Then finally, he saw the beautiful face of his wife smiling at him and he smiled back at her.

No words were exchanged as the gunmen opened fire on the table. Shattered glass flew everywhere as the bottle of liquor on the table exploded into pieces and the shot glasses hit the floor as the Matthew brothers were ripped apart one by one in a rush of bullets. The shots hit Charles square, knocking him from his chair, blowing holes the size of lemons in his chest leaving him a bloodstained mess. His eyes grew into wide, round circles as shock spread across his face and death began to creep in. He tried gasping for air but couldn't seem to catch his breath as blood filled his lungs and soaked through his tailored charcoal gray suit. The gunfire ceased and the room was filled with clouds of gunsmoke, shattered glass and splintered wood. It was a massacre. Blood flowed like a river from each bullet riddled body on the floor. Charles stared up at the ceiling, coughing up blood as the light in his eyes dimmed with each passing moment. One of the masked men stepped over him and pressed the gun to his forehead. Charles barely heard the roar of the gun before he felt a searing pain in his skull.

* * *

"We have to go back!" Emma shouted as they stood in the massive lobby of the Waldrof Astoria, "I forgot the passports."

"What?" Marion asked with a confused look on his face.

"I forgot the passports. My father has them. He picked them up for us earlier today," she explained pulling her hand away and racing back towards the steps.

Marion sighed a deep breath as he turned on his heels and chased behind her heading back up to the reception hall.

Reaching the top of the stairs and pushing open the door, Emma let out a wail when she saw the gruesome scene inside of the ballroom. The amount of blood was unreal. Blood splatter covered the walls and shattered glass glistened next to hundreds of shell casings on the floor.

Emma could hear her heart breaking as she approached the bodies of her uncles laying in a pool, about an inch thick, of crimson colored liquid. She shut her eyes in misery as tears streamed down her face.

Marion called out to Emma as he entered closely behind.

He stopped in his tracks seeing all the bodies. They had been filled with so many bullets that he couldn't tell one brother from the other. Emma's white dress had splashes of red on the bottom as she made footprints through the blood. She scanned through the bodies until her eyes landed on her father. When they did, her stomach quaked and she had to fight back the vomit in her throat. Charles's body was twitching, jumping around on the floor like a fish out of water. A stream of blood oozed from the hole in his forehead and spilled down his face.

"Daddy," Emma cried out from her heart, dropping to her knees and placing his head in her lap. Her beautiful dress turned crimson as she held her father's head and wept uncontrollably. Charles entire body began to jolt back and forth. His pleading eyes were open and focused squarely on Marion. He wanted to be put out of his misery, a mercy Marion had shown to a few soldiers in the battlefields of Vietnam. Emma seen it in her father's eyes too but didn't want to let go.

"Noooo!" she shouted at Marion her eyes piercing through him, stopping him from moving towards Charles. "Don't you dare," she challenged.

"I know it's hard but he is suffering," he regretfully tried explaining. "Look at him."

"I don't care," Emma said defiantly even as her father shook violently in her lap.

"Emma please, he's suffering. He wouldn't want to go like this," Marion pleaded.

Emma stared down at her father, caressing his face gently. He had been her whole world for so long. The first man she ever loved and the first man to love her. Her superman. She didn't want to let him go but to see him suffering ripped her apart inside.

"I love you daddy," she struggled through her tears then turned her head away as Marion slowly knelt down next to Charles.

He placed his hand over Charles' nose and mouth. Calm and poised, Marion held his hand there until Charles body stopped convulsing, then gently closed his eyelids. He rose to his feet and looked around the room at the bodies again but couldn't bear to look at Emma.

Emma was distraught and inconsolable. The anguish of losing her beloved father could only have been compounded by the deaths of her uncles. In mere seconds she had lost all of her family. She felt faint. She placed her hand over her stomach, there was life growing inside of her. A secret she hadn't even shared with Marion. She planned on surprising all the men in her life after the honeymoon with the good news. But now she regretted waiting, her father would never know his grandchild or the children that would surely follow. She looked up at Marion, he was all she had left in the world. She said a silent prayer that he would always be there to love and protect her and that he wouldn't suffer the same fate as all the other men in her life had. The room began to spin and she felt dizzy.

Marion stared at her, his heart filled with guilt. *"This is my fault,"* he thought to himself. *"I brought this on these people."* He noticed Emma was quickly becoming pale and called out to her just as she fainted.

CHAPTER 14

Marion sat with his head down next to Emma's hospital bed, silently praying as he held her hand in his lacing their fingers together. Sitting in the dimly lit room, he was consumed by guilt and filled with remorse. His plan had cost Emma everything and her family paid with their lives. Marion's broad shoulders were slumped seemingly unable to carry the burden of his actions. *"What did it profit a man to gain the world and lose his soul,"* he thought to himself as visions of the wedding massacre played in his mind. He lifted his head feeling Emma beginning to move as she stirred from her slumber.

Emma cracked her eyes as Marion caressed her hand. Although she was happy to see his face, she had so many other reasons to be sad. As those thoughts invaded her mind, her eyes filled with tears. Marion rose to his feet, sweeping her hair out of her face and wiping her tears. Emma looked up at him and fear filled her chest. She had lost so much. She couldn't bear the thought of losing him. She just wanted to hold onto him forever. She wanted him to give up the streets, not just for her but for the little life that was growing inside of her.

"You are all I have left, Marion," she said through tears. "My father, my uncles, they're all gone because of this life," Emma shook her head in disbelief. "I can't lose you too. I would rather die than to not have you."

Marion squeezed her hand reassuringly as he gazed at the love of his life. He understood her plight. Emma was broken, mind, body and spirit. She had suffered more than anyone could withstand. He saw the fear in her eyes and felt the concern in her words. No woman, no matter how accustomed they were to the workings of the underworld, would choose this life for their significant other. It was far too dangerous, but for Marion it was the only life he knew. The lawless rules of the streets were the only thing he understood and he thrived in it. He cupped her face with his hands, "You don't have anything to worry about. I'm not going anywhere," he said trying his best to ease her concerns.

"Marion," Emma said as tears fell from her eyes, as she thought about him being sent to prison or worst; gunned down by his enemies. "I know the way things are for people like us. I know our choices are limited. I'm just worried you will—" overcome by grief she was unable to finish her sentence. She knew no matter what she said it wouldn't change his mind or his path. But that path was a perilous one and that is what scared her the most.

Marion wrapped his arms around Emma as she buried her head into his chest, hoping to find comfort and a bit of peace in his warm embrace. Marion tried to lighten the mood some by switching subjects. "So, when were you gonna tell me that I'm gonna be a father?" he asked.

"How'd you know?" Emma asked as her mouth fell open in surprise.

"The doctor told me, while you were resting," Marion said with a wide smile.

For Emma, the news was still bitter sweet but she managed to smile through her tears. "Are you happy?" she questioned.

"I couldn't be happier," he answered.

Emma's face grew sad again, "I never got a chance to tell my father."

All Marion's guilt immediately returned. He stared down at the dry blood on his tuxedo and couldn't look Emma in the face again. It was a harsh reminder that the best and worst day of his life was happening simultaneously.

Emma noticed the look on his face, "Are you sure that you're happy about the news?"

"Yes," he said quickly clearing any doubt she may have. "Look who's here," he said pointing towards the door.

"Hey baby," Ms. Tina said as she entered the room. "How are you feeling?" she asked fight back her own tears.

"Ms. Tina is gonna come stay with us for a while," Marion informed Emma. "Help you out around the house with the new baby coming."

Ms. Tina tried to smile and Emma forced one but her sadness drowned out any joy she could muster.

"Ok, you need to get you some rest," Marion said. "The

doctor said the mixture of stress and fatigue is why you fainted. All this stress isn't good for you or the baby," he said as he pulled the blanket up on her. Marion looked towards the door, where Nate was now standing, then back to Ms. Tina. "Nate is gonna take you to our house," he said. "I'm staying here for the night."

Ms. Tina leaned over the bed and kissed Emma, "I'll see you soon baby," she said. Then smiled at Marion before heading out of the room.

"Marion," Emma whispered. "Promise me you'll never leave me."

"I promise," he said, kissing her on the forehead and taking a seat next to the bed. Marion locked fingers with her once again.

Emma sighed and looked away towards the window, as tears returned to her eyes and rolled down her face.

CHAPTER 15

2 Days Later

It was just after ten o'clock when Marion pulled up in front of a beautiful home in a quiet, upper-middle class neighborhood in Queens. The sweltering humidity hadn't lifted, the air was thick and hot. A dog barked in the distance as he exited the car and made his way along side of the house. He felt the gun in his waist, hidden beneath his belt and was ready for anything that came his way, although he had nothing to fear. The house belonged to Carlo Brigandi and the two of them were meeting in the Don's backyard. Covered by the shadows, away from any prying eyes.

"Anybody follow you?" Carlo asked immediately to which Marion shook his head no.

"I like you kid. And not just because of your father. I like your style. The way you carry yourself. You got balls and a silent authority about yourself," Brigandi praised. "Those are great qualities for a man to have in this business."

Marion nodded his head respectfully, appreciative of Brigandi's words. "Thank you."

"You're welcome," Brigandi said. "But it's me, who should be thanking you. That plan of yours was pure genius."

The plan he was referring to was the one Marion had devised after the murders of Goose and his cousin Josie. The conversation between Marion and Brigandi had taken place a day later. Members of the Commission needed the war between Joseph Martello and Charles Matthews to end. After Goose and Josie's death, Marion wanted revenge, he knew Jimmy was responsible but wasn't sure if the order had come from Charles or not. Either way his mind had been made up on the course of action he would take. Marion knew Carlo felt Joseph Martello was too stubborn to end the war, he also knew secretly Carlo wanted Martello dead but wanted to avoid a war within The Commission. Marion offered to deal with the problem. If Carlo helped him with his, Joseph Martello's killing would never be connected back to Brigandi.

For his part, Marion wanted the Matthews family out of the way but couldn't do it himself without risking losing Emma. So Brigandi provided him with the deadly caterers for his wedding. Both men's problems were solved and now they had a secret on one another, that forged a bond.

"Took a lot of guts to do what you did," Brigandi said.

"I had no choice," Marion admitted seriously. "After all, two kings can't occupy the same throne."

Marion Holloway was definitely the new king, Carlo admitted to himself and the streets would soon acknowledge that as well. Nothing else needed to be said. Marion nodded then headed back to his car.

Marion slid into the driver's seat and stared at himself in the rearview mirror, he was satisfied at who he saw staring back. He understood that moving forward there would be times when he'd have to be the bad guy for the greater good. He accepted that it would take a small piece of his soul every time. He knew that it may haunt him for a while but even that would lessen as time went on. Regardless of all of that, Marion knew he would do whatever had to be done, every time. His only problem now would be hiding the truth about her family from Emma and hoping that it never came back to haunt him. As Marion pulled away from the curb, he paid no attention to the car that had been following him for the past couple of days.

* * *

Across the city, inside a restaurant on the corner of East 114th Street, an informal but very necessary meeting was taking place. Carmine Perrucci and Frank Lucarelli, bosses of their families, sat across from one another enjoying a plate of spinach manicotti surrounded by their underbosses and capos. The two men sat huddled at a table in the back of the restaurant. The table was covered with small pieces of paper and receipts as they went over the books on a garment racket the two of them shared. Aside from their men and a waiter, the restaurant was empty of any patrons or employees. Carmine Perrucci shoved the empty plate away and cleared his throat. Immediately the table fell silent, the time for feasting was over. It was time to talk business.

"First, I would like to thank you for meeting with me on such short notice. The reason I called you here is about that cocksucker Brigandi," Perrucci spoke without any fear of consequence, knowing every man in the room shared his negative view of Carlo. "My gut tells me he was somehow behind Joey Martello's murder."

"Word is he used some drug dealing' nigger to do it," Lucarelli added.

"Same nigger that's been making noise over in Williamsburg," one of the capos said.

"Who is he?" Perrucci asked.

"Some spook named Marion Holloway," the capo replied.

"He's a nobody, boss," Perrucci's underboss said. "A goldfish with a shark's ego."

The men all laughed.

Frank Lucarelli didn't, he knew the Holloway name well but remained quiet on the subject.

"Fu'getabout the nigger for now," Perrucci said in a very dismissive tone. "Brigandi tried to outsmart us all. He knows you have to get The Commission's approval for a hit like the one on Martello. He broke the rules. He should pay with his life."

Every man in the room agreed.

As they exited the restaurant, each group went their separate ways. Frank Lucarelli rode in the backseat of his car, alongside his underboss. As they turned the corner he leaned over and said, "All problems start off small. Marion Holloway can't be ignored."

"You think Perrucci is underestimating him?" His underboss asked.

"Yeah, but I'm not. It took a lot of balls to pull off that Martello hit," Lucarelli acknowledged.

"You want me to have him clipped?" The underboss asked.

"Yeah but don't use any of our guys, capeesh?"

"Capeesh. I'll take care of it boss. I have someone in mind."

"Who?" Lucarelli inquired, amazed at how fast his underboss had come up with a name.

"Silvio Di Toro's kid...Mikey."

TO BE CONTINUED....

Ty Marshall

<u>More Ty Marshall Books</u>

Keys to the Kingdom

Keys to the Kingdom 2

80's Baby: When Crack Made Kings

Gold Blooded

Eat, Prey & No Love

Goodfellas

<u>Coming Soon from Ty Marshall</u>

Keys to the Kingdom 3

The Book of Rheason

The People vs. Emory Barnes

WWW.TYMARSHALLBOOKS.COM